"Have you ever [...] in a hayloft?"

Ben turned Juliana in his embrace so she could see the silver moonlight spilling through the open loft doors. "Of course, this isn't hay. It's straw. You'd have to be a masochist to sleep on hay."

"I might be willing to try, if that's the only way I could—" She choked on the words.

"Say it." He massaged her arms, raising gooseflesh. "Say anything you want."

Juliana drew in a shaky breath. "If that's the only way I could have you, Ben. The way I feel right now, I could lie on a bed of nails. I don't know what's happening to me."

She clutched the hem of her shirt and drew it smoothly over her head. "All I know is that I'm mad for you...."

His low, languid laughter skittered along her nerve endings. "You're a greedy little thing, once you make up your mind." Ben scooped her up and lay her down on a pile of straw, then began to throw off his clothing.

In exquisite anticipation, Juliana lifted her arms to him ... tinder awaiting his match.

Ruth Jean Dale is a remarkable woman. Like the heroine of *One More Chance*, she survived a brain aneurysm and fought her way out of that trauma with a vengeance. A longtime newspaper editor, Ruth launched a brilliant second career as a romance writer, with astonishing rapidity creating one gem after another for Harlequin Temptation. This is her third novel in two years, with many more to come.

In addition to being a wife, mother and grandmother, Ruth is actively involved with a prominent San Diego writers group. No one can say Ruth Jean Dale hasn't made the most of *her* second chance!

Books by Ruth Jean Dale

HARLEQUIN TEMPTATION
244–EXTRA! EXTRA!
286–TOGETHER AGAIN

One More Chance
RUTH JEAN DALE

Harlequin Books

TORONTO • NEW YORK • LONDON
AMSTERDAM • PARIS • SYDNEY • HAMBURG
STOCKHOLM • ATHENS • TOKYO • MILAN

For my daughters,
who know all about second chances....
They not only bravely endured
their mother's brain surgery
but their father's, as well.
Into each life some rain must fall,
but this is ridiculous!

Published September 1990

ISBN 0-373-25415-6

1

JULIANA ROBINSON BRACED HERSELF between the two angry men, planting a hand on the chest of each as they strained toward each other. One chest was bare and muscular. An expensively tailored suit coat and pristine white shirt covered the other.

Benjamin Ware exerted just a degree more pressure against her hand, and she felt his muscles flex beneath the warm brown skin. She turned her head sharply, intending to give him a pointed reprimand, but the challenge in his heavy-lidded blue eyes stopped her cold.

"Not only no, but *hell no*," he said in that dangerous, gravelly voice. Juliana might not even have been present, so little attention did he pay her as his gaze locked with that of Cary Goddard. "You'll get this land when hell freezes over."

The light of combat, raw edged and eager, gleamed in Ben's eyes. He wanted a fight. His whisker-stubbled jaw jutted out with an aggression that chilled her.

The voice of Cary Goddard, the man on the other end of Juliana's outstretched arms, purred past her ear. "Then prepare for a long, cold winter."

Standing in the middle of the twenty-two-point-nine acres of prime Southern California real estate in question, Juliana swung her outraged glance from one man to the other. "What's the matter with you two?" she demanded. "It's only business!"

Except it wasn't—this was something entirely different.

She'd known Ben would be difficult. Hell, Ben had *always* been difficult. He'd also given her fair warning in a letter stating succinctly that the Ware avocado ranch was no longer for sale. She'd figured this was an honest reaction on his part—either honest grief over his mother's death or honest greed. Either way, she could deal with it.

Or so she had told herself when she hounded him into this meeting. Looking at him now, she wasn't so sure.

His thick blond hair, wild and unruly as his attitude, curled around his ears and tumbled over his forehead. The silky texture did nothing whatsoever to soften his rugged features. His finely drawn lips were curled back over his teeth almost in a snarl. He looked past Juliana with an arrogance that set her teeth on edge.

"Read my lips." Ben's harsh voice broke the tight silence. "No. N-O. End of negotiations."

Cary Goddard uttered an oath. She glanced at him with alarm. Cary wasn't used to being thwarted, especially not when he'd come so close to success.

Fifty-five to Ben's forty, Cary stood six feet tall and still looked small next to Ben. Normally, his silver hair and full mustache gave him a jaunty air. At the moment he looked petulant as a spoiled child.

Juliana's arms quivered with the strain of holding off these two would-be raging bulls. Then it dawned on her that she was being used.

If they really wanted to get at each other, no mere woman—even one who stood five-eight and went to great trouble and expense to keep everything tuned and in its proper place—was going to keep them apart. She dropped her aching arms and stepped back, raking them both with her annoyed glance.

"Okay," she announced, planting her hands on her hips. "Settle it like men." Her lip curled contemptuously. "Beat the hell out of each other."

For a moment more they glared at each other. Then her sarcasm seemed to sink in and the fighting tension oozed away.

Cary crossed his arms, his expression turning cynical. "I can see we've caught you at a bad time," he said to Ben in a tone barely short of sneering. "We don't mean to intrude on your grief but we thought you'd want to honor your mother's final wishes."

"No."

Juliana heard the finality in Ben's voice, but she'd worked too long and hard on this deal to give up now. "Hear us out, Ben," she urged. "It's what your mother wanted."

"My mother's dead." Ben spoke with shocking curtness, his low voice raw edged. "It's not what I want."

"But—"

Cary cut in. "Now see here, Ware, we had a deal with your mother."

Juliana laid a restraining hand on Cary's arm. "Let me." He hesitated, and she added, "It's what you're paying me for, remember?"

He shrugged. Relieved, she turned her attention back to Ben. "There's been a lot of time and effort and money poured into this project," she said calmly. "Your mother died two days before escrow was to close, for heaven's sake! Be reasonable—do you think it's fair to back out now, without even telling us why?"

"Hell, yes!"

Ben seemed to have gained control over his hostility. Now he just looked impatient, maybe even a little scornful, as if they were wasting his time.

Juliana's lips thinned with displeasure. She'd been in real estate long enough to know how critical it was to keep cool, but Ben Ware really got her hackles up. Still, she managed to speak calmly. "What does Lillian have to say about this?"

"My sister backs me all the way."

Cary's hot, dark eyes narrowed. "Does she? It may not be quite that simple," he said. "Goddard Enterprises has already sunk a lot of bucks into this project. We may have recourse, legal or otherwise. If you're after more money..."

Ben shook his head. "That's bull. You still don't understand, do you? Money's not the issue here."

Cary's harsh grunt spoke volumes. "Money's always the issue. Let's discuss it. Reasonable men can always reach a meeting of the minds."

Cut completely out of the conversation, an exasperated Juliana looked from one to the other. This was personal, a kind of man-thing in which she had no part. But damn it, she was the professional and she didn't like being ignored.

Ben let out his breath in an explosive grunt. "I'm not interested in being reasonable." His smoky voice vibrated with passion. "I'd *give* this land away before I'd see it in your hands."

Cary surged forward again, but Juliana caught his arm. "Let me talk to Ben alone, Cary," she pleaded.

He shook her off, but Ben had already turned away to stride toward the house. For a moment, Juliana stared after him. Cary let out his breath in a disgusted snort and she looked around guiltily.

"I've about had it with that clown," he said. "I'll own this land if I have to break him to get it."

His vehemence alarmed her. "Maybe it's time to back off," she suggested. "I'm as disappointed as you are, but it is his property . . . or will be, after probate."

"A temporary situation, I can assure you." His jaws clenched, then relaxed. He gave her a quick smile. "Hey, don't look so serious. None of this will matter in a hundred years."

She grimaced. That could be taken any number of ways: to name but two, Ben could keep his land and it wouldn't matter in the long run, or Cary could wrest the land away by hook or crook, and history would be none the wiser.

She knew that in Cary's book, the end justified the means. In all fairness, she had to admit that she, too, often operated on that principle. She couldn't afford to get sanctimonious at this point.

Together they walked through the dappled shade toward Cary's sports car, their hands close but not quite touching. She barely noticed the golden February sun that warmed her—it was just a typical California winter day. She sold climate; she didn't have time to value it herself.

"I'll take one more crack at him before I leave," she promised. "Maybe he'll talk to me if you're not there, tell me what's got him so worked up."

Cary assessed her, his gaze roaming approvingly from the top of her luxuriant auburn hair, down past the jade-green dress that clung in all the right places, and on to the high-heeled pumps. A slight smile curved his lips. "If you can't get it out of him, nobody can."

He caught one of her hands and lifted it to plant a light kiss on her fingertips with their short, carefully manicured nails. "But there are a few things I can do, too. I happen to know Ware's overextended his credit to keep this place going—all on his mother's reputation, of course. The guy couldn't raise a plug nickel on his own."

She frowned. "How do you know that?"

"You'd be surprised what I know." His voice fairly dripped malice. "Mr. Ware has issued a challenge I look forward to accepting."

"Cary, don't do anything you'll regret."

"I never regret anything."

"Then don't do anything *I'll* regret."

"Hey, we're on the same team. Remember that." He laughed and gave her fingers a final squeeze. "What time shall I pick you up Saturday?"

"It starts early. Come by around six."

"I'll be there." He caressed her wrist and arm with his tapered fingers. "This will be an evening you'll never forget. I'm just sorry I have this business trip first."

She cocked her head knowingly. "Business before pleasure."

He laughed. "I had two wives who never did manage to grasp that concept. I could have saved myself a lot of grief by marrying a businesswoman."

He gave her a smile rife with promise, climbed behind the wheel of his car and started the engine. She watched him drive away with a vague feeling of unease, wondering what she'd do if he proposed to her at the Valentine Ball.

Marry him, of course. What woman in her right mind wouldn't? Rich, powerful and powerfully attractive, one of the best catches to be found anywhere.... And yet, as she walked slowly toward the house, she wondered why she hesitated at the prospect of marriage to Cary Goddard.

She hated to admit it, but after ten years of independence, she'd begun to think wistfully of having someone with whom to share her life—"someone" being a euphemism for a man. She'd been slow to admit it even to herself, but not because she'd had trouble getting over Pete. In all honesty, the divorce hadn't been that traumatic. Not for her, anyway. It had been considerably worse for him, and Paige had suffered, of course. There was no such thing as a civilized divorce when children were involved.

But Paige had survived; they all had. Paige was now a student at San Diego State. Pete was struggling to make a go of a Señor Pizza franchise, and hatching all kinds of pie-in-the-sky schemes while trying to support a second wife and two sons, Paige's half brothers.

In the meantime, Juliana had taken her father's failing real estate business and single-handedly built it into one of the most successful such enterprises in Summerhill. In her own secret heart of hearts, she frequently promised herself, "Today the city, tomorrow the county, the state, and in due time . . . the world!" It was her little joke. But she never laughed.

To her, ambition was a sacred, even noble, attribute. Neither her father nor her husband had had it, and she'd learned first-hand the truth behind the old saw that "Nice guys finish last." Maybe that's what appealed to her about Cary; he'd never finished last in his life.

She sighed and turned toward the rambling frame house, her glance skipping over the weather-beaten barn. A half dozen or so citrus trees grew here at the highest point of Buena Suerte Canyon, and terraced rows of avocado trees fell away on three sides.

Still deep in thought, she passed through the gate in the picket fence and walked toward the front door.

"You don't give up, do you?"

Her head swung around and she saw Ben standing in the open doorway of the kitchen. His impassive expression gave nothing away.

He'd put on a chambray shirt, but hadn't bothered to button it or tuck it in. Looking at him, Juliana felt an unexpected spark of interest.

Ben had been a hell-raiser as a kid, quick to anger but quicker to smile, and popular with both sexes. Somehow she found it hard to see that devil-may-care kid in the powerfully built and grim-faced man filling the doorway.

She looked him over with impersonal appreciation. His faded Levi's, worn low over his hips, revealed a lean, flat torso, washboarded with muscle. He stood with his powerful legs planted aggressively apart in a lord-of-the-manor manner.

She sighed. "Can we talk this over?"

He crossed his arms over his chest and cocked his head to one side, studying her through slitted eyes. "Sure, now that everyone's favorite land raper is gone." He moved back and gestured for her to enter.

"Are you one of those?" She stepped inside.

"One of who?"

"No-growth-ers, slow-growth-ers—whatever you want to call them." She knew what *she* usually called them, but she was trying to get on his good side, assuming he had one.

He shook his shaggy head. "Naw. I just don't like Cary Goddard or Goddard Enterprises or anything or anybody connected to him."

"Present company excluded, I hope." She favored him with a look she hoped was ingratiating.

"The jury's still out on that. Want a cup of coffee?"

"Kind of late in the day for coffee." She looked around the old-fashioned kitchen noting the cracked linoleum on the floor and faded chintz curtains at the windows. An aged dinette table with five chairs stood against one wall. A coffee cup and cereal bowl announced his less-than-appealing breakfast, sandwich scraps on a plate his lunch. Letters and mail littered the tabletop.

He gestured vaguely toward the refrigerator. "I think I might have some tomato juice."

She walked to the table and began stacking the dirty dishes. "You're not sure?"

He opened the refrigerator and extracted a tall can without a label, holding it down so he could peer at the top with its two darkly encrusted puncture holes. He shook the can, held it up and smelled the contents. He nodded. "Yeah, it's tomato juice all right."

She shook her head. "No thanks. I make it a rule never to drink anything I don't recognize at first glance."

He gave her a disapproving look and replaced the can in the refrigerator. "Where's your spirit of adventure? You might like it if you tried it." He picked up a cup off the counter and reached for the coffeepot on the stove.

"We'll never know, will we? I don't take chances when I can go with a sure thing." She placed the dirty dishes in the sink and picked up a dishcloth.

"What the hell are you doing now?" His husky voice sounded testy.

"Wiping up the sugar *somebody* spilled on the table. It'll attract ants and bugs and other undesirable elements." She washed the tabletop carefully, moving the newspapers and unopened mail out of the way. Most of the envelopes looked as if they contained bills.

"I think it already has." He gave her a sour look and sat down, plunking his cup on the table.

She tossed the cloth into the sink. "I didn't mean to hurt your feelings." She sat down across from him. "Paige says I'm an obsessive-compulsive personality."

"Paige is your kid?"

"Yes."

He drank. "She's probably right. It's sure as hell nothing to be proud of."

"It's not so bad, actually. When I see something that needs to be done, I just do it." She eyed the stack of mail in front of him.

"And you're the one who decides what needs to be done, I take it."

"Things like that tend to be obvious." She leaned back in her chair. "Damn, you haven't changed since high school. You made me crazy then and you're still doing it." She added, "Open your mail, will you?" She couldn't stand it any longer.

He grimaced and glanced down at the stack. "Hey, here's a letter from Lillian," he exclaimed, tearing open the envelope. Snatching out the sheets of paper, he began to read.

Juliana watched him, thinking that she hadn't been quite accurate. He *had* changed since high school.

Then he'd been a boy. Now he was a man.

There was something solid and commanding about him that went beyond the merely physical, although that had much to recommend it. Beneath the open folds of his shirt she could see the roping and cording of muscle each time he moved. Looking at that broad expanse of chest made her own breasts tingle and her nipples tighten.

As he read his letter she examined her reactions to him. It astonished her to acknowledge that she found him exciting. She almost never allowed herself to respond to men in sexual terms and hadn't for a very long time. She was accustomed to being in control of both situations and feelings—an impossibility when it came to sex. So she had simply decided sex was superfluous.

Other attributes were much more important in a man than sex appeal anyway, qualities like ambition and drive . . . social status and money.

She couldn't see any harm in a little innocent speculation, however, and she tried to remember what she'd heard of Ben over the years. It was precious little. He'd been married, but he'd come back to Summerhill a couple of months ago alone, so maybe he was divorced. He didn't wear a ring. She seemed to recall that he'd been a policeman, but she didn't think that's what he was doing when his mother died. Some kind of social worker? That seemed so incongruous that she had to smother a laugh.

Not that it mattered. If he were ambitious, he wouldn't be wasting his time fooling around with avocados on some of the most valuable real estate in Southern California. And yet, misguided as he appeared to be, Ben Ware was a man to reckon with.

He glanced up from the letter, his expression pleased. "Lil's promised to come visit first chance she gets. She wants to see for herself how I'm adapting to the life of a gentleman avocado rancher."

She groaned. "Give it up, will you? The gentleman part is pure fantasy. I devoutly hope you'll have come to your senses and dumped this place long before she gets here."

He raised his eyebrows in mock horror. Reading his sister's letter seemed to have put him in a much better mood. "And sell my birthright?"

"Hey, remember who you're talking to." She leaned forward, clasping her hands before her on the table. "As I recall, your folks didn't even buy this place until you were a senior in high school. You couldn't wait to blow the old homestead when you graduated. As far as I know, you never looked back."

"Words to live by—don't deal with folks who knew you when." He spoke with wry humor.

He seemed to be letting down his guard so she decided to push a little further. "Ben, take the money and run. Trust me. I shouldn't tell you this, but Cary Goddard is so obsessed with owning this land that he'll go even higher."

"Trust you. You sound like a used-car salesman." All the relaxed good humor evaporated. "My mother trusted you, I suppose." He turned the coffee cup around and around with big, competent-looking hands. He glanced up unexpectedly. "Thanks for the flowers."

She shifted uncomfortably, well aware that he'd changed the subject. "It was nothing."

"That's true. I'm just being polite. But you also came to the funeral. I appreciated that, and so did Lil."

She wanted to wriggle beneath his candid gaze. Her motives had been *fairly* pure, but not pure enough for her to face him with a completely clear conscience. "Ben, please don't put this on a personal level," she said, feeling uncomfortable. "Friendship just doesn't mix with business."

"I'm no more interested in relating on a 'personal level,' as you put it, than you are, Juliana Maria Malone Robinson. But you can't deny we go back a long way, you and me." He looked disgusted, as if she'd disappointed him somehow.

"Good." She spoke with finality, even as her stomach clenched. "Let's talk some business."

The shrill ring of the wall-mounted telephone cut her off. Impatiently she settled back as he rose to answer it. She saw him frown, heard him mutter, "Yeah, she's here."

He offered her the phone and she took it with a shrug that said, "I can't imagine." The extra-long curly cord stretched to accommodate the exchange.

"Hello?"

"Hi, Juli. It's me, Pete."

"What do you want?"

"Now, don't freak. I wonder...I wonder if you've given any more thought to what we talked about last week? You said you'd get back to me and . . . Well, I thought maybe you'd tried and missed me."

She'd always hated that wheedling tone. Her jaws tightened, but Ben was watching so she spoke calmly. "There's nothing to think about, Pete. Frozen yogurt is on its way out. A combination pizza-yogurt store won't fly. It's not a good investment."

A brief silence, and then he flared, "Well, what if I think it is?"

"You're entitled to your opinion, however erroneous. Just don't expect me to invest my hard-earned money in another of your schemes."

"You didn't lose a penny on that deal."

"I didn't make a penny, either."

"I don't suppose the opinions of my banker or my accountant would mean anything to you?"

"You suppose correctly."

"How about ten years of marriage?" he flared. "Naw— that wouldn't mean diddly. Let me speak to Ben."

As much as she hated to do it, she passed the receiver back to Ben. "He wants to talk to you."

Ben's side of the conversation wasn't very revealing. A few "a-huhs," several glances in Juliana's direction and a final "Yeah, we'll talk later." He hung up the receiver.

He looked at her impassively, his square chin characteristically out-thrust. "Jeez, you're one tough cookie," he said.

"What did Pete say about me?" Damn—she hadn't wanted to stoop to asking.

"Not much. Something about keeping my back against the wall."

She glared at him. "And you believe him?"

"Well, hey... if it swims like a shark and bites like a shark..." He shrugged and gestured, palms up. "I just heard you give the shaft to a man you used to sleep with, the man who fathered your only child, and you didn't blink an eye. Yeah, I probably believe him."

Her growing anger surprised her. She knew she was considered driven and difficult in some circles, but no one had ever dared speak to her so bluntly. Well, you had to be tough in business or you ended up on welfare or close to it, like a few people she could name. "It was a bad investment," she said somewhat petulantly. "Sentiment has no cash value. I could have lost money on the deal."

He raised his brows, the picture of innocence. "I heard you had more money than you'd ever need if you never made another cent."

"And I wouldn't if everybody was like you."

"But how much is enough? You can only spend it so fast."

"Give it a rest, Ben." She tried to lighten things up. "Don't you know you can never be too rich or too thin?"

"That's the dumbest piece of bull.... What a stupid thing to say. I'm beginning to think a little human compassion wouldn't hurt you a helluva lot."

"That's not the issue." She tried to stare him down and failed. "You know who finishes last, don't you?"

"Yeah. Nice guys like your father and your ex-husband."

That observation stunned her. She snatched up her purse. "You mind if I smoke?" she demanded brusquely, surprised and discomfited that she'd let him upset her this much.

"As a reformed smoker, I'm not crazy about the idea."

She gave him a so-what glance and lit up, drawing the smoke deep into her lungs. "I'm not hooked, you know. I'll quit one of these days." She exhaled slowly. "I've cut way back," she added, trying to justify what she privately considered a weak and filthy habit, "but every once in a while I just have to give in."

"Hell, it's probably your only weakness of the flesh." His scorn stung her.

The usually soothing effects of the nicotine weren't reaching her today. "Are you trying to make a point?"

He shrugged. "Only that you seem to know the price of everything and the value of nothing."

"Hey, that's very original. I come here to buy land and I get platitudes." She pulled up a sheet of newspaper and tapped ashes onto it. She started to rise but her equilibrium seemed suddenly out of kilter. She swayed and caught herself with her hands on the tabletop. "I'm . . . I'm . . ."

"Take it easy. This is a purely intellectual discussion. I've decided to explain to you why I won't sell this land to Goddard, now or ever."

"It's . . . I—" She looked at him through a halo of light that wavered and shimmered around him. She tried to form a coherent sentence in her brain, in her mouth, and failed.

He stared down at his hands on the table, a faint, grim smile playing around his lips. "The direct approach leaves you speechless, I see." He hesitated. "I don't suppose you've ever needed a second chance."

"Why I—I—" Something exploded in her skull and she blinked and gasped for breath. It felt as if the top of her head had been torn away. Agony, too intense and blinding and all-pervasive to be labeled pain, ripped through her, leaving no cell of her body untouched.

"Well, I do and this is it." He looked out the window, his expression bleak. "I should have come home a long time ago but I couldn't—I wasn't ready to face all the unfulfilled potential. Maybe I'm still not ready, but I promised my mother I'd try. If I go down this time, I'll never get up again."

His words made no sense to her; they were so much noise. Nausea rose in her throat. She couldn't see, the light hurt her eyes and they refused to focus. She was going to be sick right here at—where the hell ever she was. Coherent thoughts could not surface through the drowning sensation that accompanied the hellish pain hammering inside her skull.

His voice continued, expressionless. "I'm willing to work, sacrifice, whatever the hell it takes. But I don't want that slimy bastard Goddard nosing around here anymore. He's like the snake waving the apple under my nose and saying 'Try it, you'll like it!' With that kind of money there's not a damned thing to keep me straight. I'd be back in the gutter with a vodka bottle in my hand before you could say 'idle rich.' Hell, he knows what he's doing—he sent a private investigator to find out."

The cigarette fell from her numb fingers and bounced off the table and onto the floor. *I'm dying.* Just like that, she knew it. Nobody could survive this. She would die and never even know what killed her. Had she been shot? Had someone fired a bullet into her head?

"Juliana? Juliana, what is it?"

The voice meant nothing. Nothing meant anything except this debilitating agony. She lifted her hands to her head and pressed, her lips parting in a silent scream.

She'd always been a fighter, but she couldn't fight this. Her eyes rolled back in her head and she toppled over in groggy borderline consciousness.

2

BEN REACHED HER as she collapsed. He'd been a policeman, he'd seen people die, he'd felt pain, witnessed pain and even caused pain, but he had never seen anything strike like this.

For a moment he stood in the middle of his kitchen, holding her in his arms and wondering what the hell he ought to do. His own inadequacy overwhelmed him.

He could try to bring her around. For a moment he toyed with that idea, even though he knew he was stalling. He just didn't want to take her to the hospital. People went into those places and never came out—not alive, anyway.

His arms tightened spasmodically and he stared down at her. Against the frame of that thick copper hair, her face looked completely bloodless. She seemed unconscious, maybe in some kind of coma. But then she groaned and her eyelids flickered; for a moment he stared into pinpoint pupils before she went slack again.

Gone was the self-satisfied superiority he'd found so irritating in her earlier, swept away by the pain as her hand had swept away the crumbs from his table. She looked exposed and vulnerable now, and he did not like being a party to it. Her fallibility was none of his concern.

He'd take her to the hospital and let the doctors worry about her. But still he hesitated, immobilized by memory.

He hated hospitals. People died in hospitals. His wife and son had died in a hospital while he paced the waiting room trying to bargain for their lives with an unreasonable god. He'd be damned if he'd go through that again, not with this woman, not with anyone.

He glared down at her, something very like hatred surging up to choke him. Why did this have to happen here? He didn't want to accept responsibility for her or for anyone ever again. He refused to get involved.

She groaned and her fingers plucked ineffectually at his shirt. If he didn't get medical help for her pronto it would be too late—he felt sure she would die. Regardless of his misgivings, he realized he had no choice.

Tightening his grip on her, he barreled to the doorway and through it, heading for his pickup at a trot. Get her to a hospital and he could wash his hands of her, let someone else worry. He put her in the passenger seat and fastened the seat belt. She whimpered, but didn't open her eyes. He was thankful for that. He didn't want to confront that naked suffering again.

Would she die before he could get her some help? His heart hammered erratically in his chest. *No, damn it!* He was committed now—not through choice, through necessity. Her life depended upon him. He groaned. People who depended on him tended to end up dead.

Driving like a maniac through the hills and canyons, he talked to her without really knowing he did so.

"You've got a hell of a nerve, barging into my house and keeling over. Jeez, I'm just an innocent bystander. Why didn't you give that creep, Goddard, the honor of saving your life?"

She groaned. Ben swallowed hard. "So help me God, if you die before I get you to emergency—!" He gripped the steering wheel so hard his knuckles whitened. "Hang on, damn you—it's not much farther."

He laughed, a harsh, dissonant sound in the small cab of the vehicle. "Suffering builds character, dammit. Looks like you're gonna have more damn character than you'll know what to do with when this is over.

"Just don't die on me. Don't even *think* about dying— *You hear me?*"

THE EMERGENCY ROOM DOCTOR hesitated in the wide doorway. Ben, alone in the hospital waiting room, sprang to his feet, his mouth dry and his hands icy and shaking.

"Dr. Lindeman? I'm Ben Ware. I brought Mrs. Robinson in?" Even those few words took an enormous effort.

"Oh, yes. Thought for a minute there you'd gone."

The two men shook hands.

Ben licked his lips, afraid to ask about her. He should have left the minute the doctors took over, gone to a bar and steadied his nerve with a good stiff drink. Why the hell was he still here? He cleared his throat and forced himself to speak. "How's Juliana doing, Doctor? What's wrong with her?"

The young doctor pursed his lips. He countered the questions with one of his own: "Her daughter's not here yet?"

Ben's stomach lurched and a muscle jumped in his jaw. "I asked Juliana's secretary to meet the girl at home and bring her over. She's a student at San Diego State."

"Okay. As soon as she arrives—"

The doctor was already turning away. Ben clamped a hand around the man's forearm and squeezed—not as hard as he wanted to, but hard enough.

"Dammit, Doc, I gotta know what's going on."

The raw emotion must have pierced the doctor's preoccupation. He looked up quickly, then hesitated as if considering. "We're afraid it may be meningitis," he said finally. "We're running tests and should know soon."

"But—" Ben felt completely adrift. "Meningitis... that's serious."

Dr. Lindeman's arched brows provided verification. "Mrs. Robinson's condition is extremely grave."

"When can I see her?" He didn't know why he had asked that. He didn't want to see her, not really. If the doctor didn't think she was going to make it, why risk further involvement?

"Just what is your relationship to the patient?" The doctor's sharp eyes pinned Ben down.

Well, what was it? Old friend? Business acquaintance? Adversary? No self-respecting sawbones would let any of those into the room of a woman on the verge of death.

"Fiancé," Ben said curtly, the lie heavy on his tongue. "We were together when it happened."

"I'm sorry." The doctor's manner warmed noticeably. "Look, as soon as her daughter arrives have one of the nurses track me down. We should know something by then, and you two might as well hear it together."

Dr. Lindeman patted Ben on the shoulder and hurried out of the waiting room. For a moment Ben stood there, shoulders slumped. A middle-aged couple entered, their faces tense with worry. The man half supported the woman, who looked up at him with tears in her eyes.

Ben turned toward the window. He hated this. Damn, he hated this! He clenched his hands into impotent fists and gritted his teeth until his jaw ached. But he couldn't hold back the memories....

THE GUY ROBBED A BANK, they said, and was trying to make his getaway. With San Francisco's finest in hot pursuit, he ran a traffic light and plowed into the side of a station wagon.

The ensuing explosion killed the fugitive and a twelve-year-old boy riding in the station wagon. The driver of the wagon died, too, but not right away...that would have been too clean, too easy.

Melanie Ware lay in a coma. Ben, her husband of fourteen years, paced the hospital corridors and waited...and waited. Her parents came over from Stockton, but their presence made it even harder, because they blamed Ben for everything. Why, he couldn't imagine, except that he'd married their daughter. All he knew was that her mother turned her face away when he entered the room.

His son was buried and Ben wept. Then he returned to the hospital and waited some more.

He knew things were going badly because everyone was so nice to him. Nurses gave him comforting smiles and pitying glances while doctors shook their heads and patted him on the shoulder. Visiting hours meant nothing; he came and went as he pleased, spending at least twenty of every twenty-four hours at the hospital.

Finally the neurologist took Ben aside and explained that it was time to talk about taking Melanie off life support.

"No!" Ben recoiled in horror. He had never given up.

"I know this is difficult," the doctor said gently. "Rest assured, we'd never do anything without making absolutely certain that her brain is no longer functioning."

"Then you're not a hundred percent sure." Hope really did spring eternal.

"Mr. Ware, I'm ninety-nine-point-nine percent sure right now. If we unhook the machines, her heart may continue to pump for minutes, even hours or days. But there is no pain response or gag reflex. She has a flat-line

EEG. Mr. Ware, from my perspective, Melanie is already dead."

He paused. Ben said nothing, just stared stupidly, trying to absorb the finality of the situation.

"She carried an organ donor card," the doctor said gently. "If we're going to be able to use her kidneys, they'll have to be taken soon."

"No! You're not going to cut up my baby!" Melanie's mother had caught the doctor's last sentence and she threw herself at Ben. He fell back but not before her nails raked his face, leaving red tracks down one cheek.

Melanie's father restrained his sobbing wife, but her assault seemed to pull Ben out of his stupor, as if the drawing of blood had somehow brought him back to consciousness.

He gave the order to detach Melanie from the respirator; even her parents had to agree finally that Melanie was gone, and had been virtually from the moment of impact. The hatred in her mother's eyes burned into Ben's back as he walked away from the intensive care unit for the last time . . . and right into the nearest bar.

He stayed drunk for twenty-four hours, sobered up for Melanie's funeral, resigned from the San Francisco P.D. and started drinking again. . . .

"MR. WARE? Mr. Ware, where is my mother?"

Ben opened his eyes and stared into the frightened face of Paige Robinson. He frowned and blinked; for a moment he thought he was seeing things.

She was the image of her mother at about the same age, the age when Ben had known her best. Brown hair curled softly around Paige's shoulders and big hazel eyes stared out of an oval face. She pressed her lips together, but not before he saw them tremble.

"You're Juliana's daughter," he said, his voice even more gruff than usual. "I'd know you anywhere, Paige."

She frowned and glanced over her shoulder at the woman who followed. He'd known Stella Davis for years. She'd been a friend of his sister's.

Stella put an arm around the girl's shoulders. "Ben and your mama go way back," she said gently.

Paige nodded. "I just want to see my mother," she said in that same stiff voice. "I don't understand what's happened. She was fine this morning, not sick or anything. Mother doesn't even have *colds*, for heaven's sake. How can she be . . . here?" The girl gestured helplessly at nothing in particular.

Looking at Juliana's daughter, Ben thought of his own child, dead these three long years. The stark horror he'd felt then showed now on the girl's dazed face. He longed to comfort her, didn't know how, so he tried to speak with calm authority. "The doctors are running tests now. They'll be able to tell us something soon."

Paige recoiled. "Us? Now that I'm here, you don't have to stay, Mr. Ware." She spoke with great dignity. "I appreciate all you've done, but you're not needed."

Don't have to stay? Did she think this was his idea of a good time? he wondered. His outraged glance slammed into her, and her measured flow of words ceased abruptly. She caught her breath and took a step back.

The arrival of a doctor in surgical greens defused the tense moment. "Robinsons?"

Ben and Stella looked at Paige.

"I'm Paige Robinson. How is my mother? Can you tell me what's wrong with her?"

"That we can, little lady." The doctor gestured to a grouping of chairs and everyone moved obediently to sit.

"I'm Dr. Crow and I'm a neurosurgeon. We've performed a number of tests on your mother." He patted Paige's hand.

"Is it bad?" Her lips looked stiff and white.

"It's not good. We've done a CAT scan and an angiogram and we know now that your mother has suffered an intracranial hemorrhage caused by an aneurysm. That's—"

"Oh, dear God!" Stella's shocked exclamation brought them all swinging around. She looked stricken, but recovered quickly. "I'm sorry. Please go on."

The doctor nodded. "Yes, well an aneurysm is a weakness in the wall of an artery. It can balloon without warning and rupture very suddenly, as in your mother's case. When the rupture isn't too large we get what we call a warning bleed, and we can go in and clip the artery."

Relief flooded Paige's face and Ben turned his head, unable to handle such vulnerability.

"Then she'll be all right!"

"We hope so. We're doing everything we can, but she's not out of the woods yet. At least we have reason to hope." The doctor patted her hand again and stood up. "We'll have to get her into surgery as quickly as possible. If you'd like to see her before—"

"Oh, yes!" Paige jumped to her feet, Stella and Ben following suit.

"Down the hall and turn left." Dr. Crow pointed. "Tell the nurse at the station in front of the double doors that I sent you."

Paige gave him a distracted nod and hurried out, Stella at her heels. Ben moved to follow, but Dr. Crow stopped him.

"You're her fiancé, right?"

Ben barely hesitated over the lie. "That's right."

"I didn't want to say too much in front of the girl—" Dr. Crow's glance indicated the door through which Paige had just disappeared. "But you have a right to know, Mr. Ware. Juliana may not make it."

Juliana. The doctor spoke of her as if she were an old friend, Ben thought. And in some ways, he must know her better than anyone else. He knew her from the inside out.

The doctor waited patiently. Ben's initial shock passed and the doctor went on.

"We're getting very little pain response. Her pupils are dilated and her neck is stiff, reflexes almost nil. We did a lumbar puncture and found blood in the spinal fluid—a cerebral angiogram pinpointed the aneurysm. Mr. Ware, are you all right?"

Ben *wasn't* all right, not even close it it. A harrowing sense of déjà vu threatened to swamp him. Cold sweat broke out on his forehead—*he needed a drink!* It took every ounce of willpower he possessed to force a curt nod. "She's gotta pull through, Doc," he croaked.

The doctor gave Ben a measured glance. "We'll do our best, but her situation is extremely grave. I must stress that. If there's anyone else who should be contacted— parents, grandparents, anyone at all—now's the time to do it." He paused and then added, "You can use the phone in my office."

"I—I'll check with Paige."

"Do that." Dr. Crow gave Ben's shoulder a supportive squeeze, the same professional comfort he'd offered Paige. "You'll want to see her before we take her to surgery. Come along."

The doctor led Ben through the gleaming corridors of the hospital and every step drew him further back into a past he'd struggled to forget. He had no business even being here, passing himself off as something he wasn't.

A gurney wheeled sharply out a room ahead and he saw Juliana, strangely isolated amidst the medical personnel and the dripping I.V. bottles and the sheets and drapes that covered and surrounded and all but buried her. He had a quick impression of her face, white as paper, and then he lost sight of her as the medics rushed the gurney down the hall, hustling as if their lives depended upon it.

Or hers.

"Damn!" Dr. Crow started forward, giving Ben a final wave of one hand. "Thought I'd get you here in time— sorry."

Ben stood there helplessly. Paige appeared in the doorway. He met her angry, frightened gaze.

"This is all your fault," she said in a quivering voice, her dry, burning eyes boring into him. "Are you happy with what you've done?"

He felt as if she'd kicked him in the gut; all the breath whooshed out of him and he stared at her blankly. All her fear and anger focused on him.

"Mother was worried about meeting with you today. You must have been just awful to cause something so horrible to happen to her!"

"Paige, no!" Stella appeared in the doorway behind the girl. "You're wrong. Your mother was—*is*—a professional. Things like that don't even faze her."

"You're the one who's wrong, Stella." Paige clenched her hands into fists at her sides. She stepped closer to Ben and stared challengingly up into his eyes. "Why don't you say something?" she raged. "This is your fault—admit it!"

He couldn't argue; maybe she was right.

At the very least, he was more culpable in Juliana's peril than in his wife's—he'd *been* there when Juliana was stricken. Maybe there was something he should have done but didn't, or shouldn't have done and did.

They were drawing curious glances from medical personnel. As if of one mind, they turned back toward the waiting room.

Ben found his voice as they walked down the endless corridors. "Maybe it is my fault," he said, thinking aloud more than anything else.

"Nonsense," Stella said stoutly. "That's not what causes an aneurysm to form, or to rupture."

"Then what does?" Paige demanded.

Stella led them into the waiting room and turned toward the stiff-faced girl. "An aneurysm isn't something that happens to you. It's more like...like something you're born with. Like a weak heart."

Paige snorted. "My mother is healthy as a horse. She's never been sick a day in her life. Something or somebody *caused* this." She glared at the older woman. "So what makes you such a big expert?"

She didn't wait for an answer. Turning her back, she marched to the window, her shoulders stiff. Stella started to follow, but Ben put a hand on her arm and shook his head.

"Leave her alone for a minute," he said, in control of himself again. "Stella, the surgeon suggested that if there's anyone else who should be called about this, we do it now."

"Oh, dear Jesus." Her face quivered as if ready to crumple, and quick tears sprang to her eyes. "You're not saying...?"

Ben nodded. "It's serious, real serious. That's all I know."

"Ben, what Paige said...she's wrong. This isn't your fault."

Nice try, he thought. "Thanks. I hope you're right."

At the window, Paige whirled, her expression challenging. "I'm going to call Daddy," she announced as if she expected someone to argue with her. "He'll want to be here."

Sure he will, Ben thought. Peter would be eager to stand vigil at the bedside of the woman who not only divorced him but turned him down flat when he tried to put the touch on her a few hours ago.

But regardless of past problems, Pete showed a lot of class. He arrived just as Dr. Crow got out of surgery.

"So far so good." The doctor sounded cheerful, although he looked tired. His surgical cap was wet with sweat and his face gleamed with it. "We'll be moving her into the recovery room and then you'll be able to see her. But only for a minute." His glance encompassed all of them. "At least, some of you."

Pete asked the question Ben couldn't: "What're her chances, Doc?"

Dr. Crow looked around at the solemn little group. "I'll level with you. Large hemorrhages are fatal within a few days in half the cases. To break that down, twenty percent die before they ever make it to the emergency room and thirty percent die within a couple of weeks."

Paige's stricken glance swung from the doctor's face to her father's. "But—but that's awful!"

The doctor looked grim. "I agree, young lady. And even of those who make it, fewer than half survive without disabling neurologic problems. The aftereffects range from total disability to complete recovery for a few lucky ones. But some degree of impairment usually remains, including dysphasia."

Paige wrung her hands together frantically. "Dys-what? I don't even know what that is."

"It's simply the breakdown of language." As he spoke, the doctor gently drew her hands into his and held them still. "Dysphasia is a disturbance in the language function following injury to the brain. It can affect talking, understanding, reading, writing, mathematics, memory, that sort of thing, in any degree and any combination."

"Oh, my God." Paige's voice was a whisper.

The doctor continued hurriedly. "On the bright side, a lot of patients do make a reasonable degree of functional recovery—"

"Reasonable degree!" She looked as if he'd struck her in the face. She glanced at her father in mute appeal.

Pete slipped an arm around her waist. "Hey, don't worry, baby. The doc's talking about *people*, not your mom. There's no way this is going to get Juliana down for long. That's a promise."

Pete spoke with absolute certainty. Ben drew strength from it even as he saw Paige do the same.

"That's the spirit." Dr. Crow took a step toward the door. "If there are no more questions—"

"I have a question, Doctor." Everyone glanced in surprise at Stella, who'd been silent up to that point. "What caused this? Could it have happened because she got upset or excited or something like that?"

"Everybody always wants to know 'why,'" Dr. Crow said plaintively. "I can't answer that. These ruptures can occur anytime, totally without warning. In Juliana's case, it was almost certainly congenital—that means it wasn't caused by tension or a blow or anything like that. The potential was always there, ticking away, like a time bomb in her brain. Today it detonated. The good Lord knows why—I don't."

"Then," Stella said clearly, "Ben may have saved her life."

Dr. Crow shrugged and glanced at Ben. "Well, sure, I suppose so. You never know. Sometimes these things occur when people are alone and they lie for hours—that sure doesn't help. So the fact that she wasn't alone when it happened was certainly in her favor."

Paige's face crumpled and the first tears Ben had seen her shed slid down her cheeks. She looked at him. "I'm sorry." She mouthed the words more than spoke them.

She extended a trembling hand. He hesitated for just a fraction of a second, then took it in his own. He felt emotion tighten the back of his throat and he swallowed hard.

BEN AND PETE sat in the hospital cafeteria, drinking bitter coffee, waiting to be summoned to Juliana's bedside. Paige wasn't taking any chances. She'd refused to leave the waiting room, so Stella had taken up a tray.

Pete screwed up his thin face in a grimace. He shifted his lanky frame and picked up his cup. "This stuff tastes like battery acid," he declared cheerfully.

Ben listened without hearing; he sipped his coffee without tasting, wishing it were something a helluva lot stronger. "You really think she'll make it?"

"Hell, yes! I'm not so sure about you, though."

"Me?" Ben leaned back in his chair.

"Man, you look like death warmed over. And you didn't even like her when she was well."

When Pete and Juliana started dating in high school, Ben had been openly scornful. For the while the two friends had been on the outs, but Ben had pulled back once he realized the relationship was serious.

Now Ben shrugged. "All I meant to do was drop her off at emergency and split, but I kinda got sucked in. If I leave now, it's like...like walking out in the middle of the movie. You may not like the flick, but you paid your money and you want to know how it turns out. What's your excuse? After what you said about her on the phone earlier. . . ."

"Yeah, well, I was mad." Peter looked down into his cup sheepishly. "Juliana's not so bad, but I really came for Paige."

"She's a great kid," Ben said, meaning it. "Strong."

"Thanks." Pete grinned. "So . . . you gonna sell out to Goddard?"

Ben's eyes narrowed. "No chance."

Pete shook his head and arched his brows. "I don't get it. You're sitting on a gold mine out there. It's not like you always dreamed of being a farmer."

How to explain? Ben picked up his cup and stared down into the dregs. "I don't need money, Pete. At least I don't need *big* money. I just need enough to keep the place going."

"Why, pal? Why's this so important to you?"

Ben looked at the simple, honest face of his oldest friend. They'd grown apart over the past twenty years, but there was still a lot of mutual caring. "It's a question of self-respect," he said finally. "I've got to make something turn out right. That's what I'm hanging on for, not avocados."

That's also why he was hanging around the hospital, he realized with a start—waiting for something to turn out right. *If she's okay, I'll be okay.* Frightened by the thought, he tossed the last of the coffee down his throat and stood up. His mind and muscles responded sluggishly.

He was tired, really tired. He'd put in the equivalent of a full day's work before the confrontation that preceded Juliana's collapse. Since then, he had functioned at a level of tension that left him completely wrung out.

The truth was, he owed her nothing. She was nothing to him. He might as well go home . . . just as soon as he saw for himself that she was alive and likely to remain so.

The doctor let Ben, Pete and Paige into ICU a few minutes later. A bank of monitors surrounded Juliana's bed with blips and bleeps of light and sound. She lay with her head swathed in bandages, surrounded and connected to tubes and lines with medical paraphernalia. More tubes, held in place by white tape, trailed from each nostril.

She looked unbelievably fragile, translucent skin stretched taut over the jutting bones of her face, and as still as a wax stature. It never entered Ben's mind that she might be conscious. He hung back a little as Paige approached the bedside cautiously. She leaned down and whispered, "Mama? It's me, Paige."

To Ben's astonishment, Juliana's eyelids fluttered, then lifted slowly. The very faintest of smiles touched her chalky lips. "Hi...honey," she murmured, her voice reedy. "Think you could...get me...a cigarette? They're right there in...the lower left-hand...desk drawer."

Her eyes drifted closed. Paige looked up, her expression betraying her terror. Her father slipped an arm around her shoulder and his glance met Ben's.

They must all share the same fears, Ben thought as he turned away, but they were afraid to acknowledge them out loud.

Was she going to make it? And if she did, would she come all the way back?

3

A LOT OF BUCKS, a lot of bucks, a lot of bucks. Money's always the issue—no flowers in here! This is ICU... it'll all be the same in a hundred years.

Cary's voice, inside her head, going round and round and round in awareness as ethereal as cotton candy. And another voice—whose?—*You came to the funeral... I appreciated that. My mother's dead. Dead—no! My mother's going to be fine!*

She tried to clear out all the wisps in her brain, chase away the voices, but always they came back. *I came here to buy land and I get platitudes.* But where was "here?" Not a nice place, apparently. *Boy, she's really tough! Look at the way she's hung on since that second surgery. Tough cookie.... If it swims like a shark and bites like a shark... you give the shaft to a man you used to sleep with....*

A bald-faced lie—she didn't used to sleep with anyone except Pete and that was long ago and far away. *Ten years of marriage didn't mean diddly.*

Why was Pete angry with her? What had she ever done to him? That's what she got for dealing with people who knew her when. *How much money is enough? You can only spend it so fast... fast. Get a doctor in here, fast— something's wrong.... I'm beginning to think a little human compassion wouldn't hurt you a helluva lot.*

Ben, that's who it was, Ben what's-his-name. She relaxed, a major battle won. But the voices never stopped.

The price of everything and the value of nothing—do you think she's waking up now?

We go back a long way, you and me, a long way, a long way... my second chance... She got the second dose in at two. Haven't you ever needed a second chance—second dose—second chance? It's infected—she's on her way back to surgery... Never look back, never look back.

"Name ten animals, Juliana."

"Aardvark, uhhh... platypus...."

"Very funny."

I may have lost my mind but not my sense of humor. Pleasure before business—business before pleasure.... I'll have this land if I have to break him—when hell freezes over! I won't sell, now or ever.

My God, Juliana, what have they done to you? I'm sorry, I didn't mean...it's just such a shock. I'm sorry, I'm truly sorry— Jeez, look at these bruises. Who's been starting the I.V.s around here, Godzilla?

JULIANA'S EYES SNAPPED OPEN. "Where am I?" she asked very clearly. "What's happened to me?"

Ben and Paige looked at each other and Ben saw his own elation mirrored on the girl's face. He grinned in pure relief and she grinned back.

"What are you doing here, Ben?" Juliana's frown took in the entire room. "For that matter, what am I doing here? Is this a hospital? Paige, answer me."

Paige's laughter sparkled. "Welcome back, Mama. Yes, you're in the hospital. Don't you remember?"

"Of course I remember." Juliana fixed her daughter with a stern gaze that held absolutely no comprehension. She lay quietly for several minutes, her expression a study in concentration. Finally she said tentatively, "I was at *his* place with Cary."

Ben nodded encouragement, trying to keep the wide, silly smile off his face. She was lucid. He'd wondered if this day would ever come.

"That's right." Paige sat in a chair by the bed and stroked Juliana's arm, above the IV tube that dripped unceasingly through the needle into her hand. "What else do you remember?"

Juliana closed her eyes and frowned; her effort to remember was almost palpable. "I guess I left?"

"You collapsed. Ben brought you to the emergency room."

"Oh. I remember. I had a headache."

"Yes. Does your head hurt now?"

Juliana frowned. "No."

She raised her free hand. When her fingers touched the gauze wrapping around her head, she flinched, and Ben saw panic in her eyes.

"What's happened to me? I—I'm a little confused."

"You had brain surgery, Mama." Paige's voice trembled, as if she were on the verge of losing it. "For an aneurysm. Three times."

Paige had been so brave for so long, but now tears gathered in her eyes and spilled down her cheeks. Juliana didn't seem to notice, and it suddenly occurred to Ben that her eyesight might have been affected by what she'd been through.

"Brain surgery! I don't believe it."

"It's true. After they fixed the aneurysm, you weren't coming along very well so they operated again to put in what they called a . . . a shunt, to drain away fluids—"

"In my *brain*?"

Juliana seemed about to panic, as if all of this were news to her. Yet she'd been in and out of consciousness from the very beginning, talking to them although not always rationally. In fact, not often rationally, Ben amended.

Paige continued to stroke her mother's arm. "The shunt got infected, so they had to operate again to take it out. But now everything's going to be just fine, it really is."

For a moment Ben thought Juliana would let it rest there, but then she asked, in a frightened voice, "The last thing I remember is sitting in *his* kitchen. How long have I been here?"

Paige licked her lips, her smile tremulous. "Three weeks, Mama. You've been here three weeks."

Hell, they're both going to break down, Ben thought. He leaned forward. "Three *bad* weeks. You were better off wherever the hell you were."

Her lips still trembled but a little fire appeared in her eyes. "What are *you* doing here, B-Ben Ware?"

"I wish I knew," he said, disgusted. "I guess I feel responsible. I don't know why—I just happened to be standing there fat, dumb and happy when you keeled over in my kitchen."

"You're not fat," she objected faintly. Her eyelids drifted closed and she slept.

Ben's astonished gaze met Paige's. They burst into simultaneous laughter.

I wasn't happy, either, he thought. *But I sure as hell was dumb—still am, apparently.*

JULIANA SAT on the edge of the hospital bed, staring with dull hostility at the tray of food. She swayed slightly, feeling dizzy and disoriented. "I want a cigarette," she burst out. She shoved the bedside table away, slopping soup over the edge of a plastic bowl.

Ben shoved it back again. "Stop being a pain in the butt and eat."

Responding to the tone of command, she picked up her fork and stabbed at a gray lump of . . . something, maybe meat. "This stuff's awful. You wouldn't like it if you had to—"

"But I don't have to—you do. Shut up and eat."

She gave him a furious glance and lifted the fork to her mouth. She had no idea what she was eating. She halfway suspected the doctors had removed her taste buds. Everything blurred together on her tongue and tasted exactly the same, which was to say, awful. She picked up the buttered roll. "I want to go home." Her voice trembled. "Where's Paige? Tell her I'm ready now."

"I explained that to you." He spoke with exaggerated patience. "She's trying to catch up on her school work. She's missed a lot of classes, spending so much time here."

"Oh." She didn't remember him telling her anything of the kind. She dropped the roll onto her tray.

He picked up the roll and shoved it back into her hand. "I promised Paige you'd eat a decent supper and, by damn, you're going to. Take a bite."

She did. It was easier than arguing.

JULIANA ROLLED OVER. Even half-asleep, she remained acutely aware on some level of the need for caution to avoid disturbing the I.V. needle taped to her hand. She'd grown accustomed to the stiffness in her neck and she moved with care.

Yawning, she lifted her free hand to rub her eyes, then stroked across her forehead and over the top of her head. Her fingers did not encounter the gauze helmet she'd come to accept; instead she felt stubble.

She sat bolt upright in the bed.

Paige leaped to her side. "Mama, what's wrong?"

"My hair. What have they done to my hair?" Juliana pressed the heels of both palms against her temples, fingers splayed across the shaven remains of a once-glorious head of hair. The most awful sense of betrayal choked her, and yet she didn't feel surprise, exactly.

Paige tried to pry her mother's hands away from her head. "We explained all that to you, remember? Three days ago when they moved you from intensive care—"

"They didn't have to shave my head just because they moved me." None of this made sense to Juliana; all she knew was that she was virtually bald, a situation profoundly shocking.

"Hi. You up for company?"

Juliana jumped at the unexpected voice and twisted around. Ben stood grinning in the doorway. Without waiting for an invitation, he entered.

He carried a foil-wrapped pot of daisies and looked around for a place to set it. Every available surface was covered with plants and flowers and get-well cards.

Humiliation laced with anger washed over her. She had no place to hide, so she just turned away and sank back down on the bed, closing her eyes. When she finally opened them, everyone was gone.

BEN AND PAIGE walked down the hospital corridor, his arm around her shoulder. During the weeks of waiting, they'd grown closer then he would ever have believed possible—closer than he should ever have allowed.

He'd have been proud to be her father, he thought with melancholy regret. She was strong and gutsy—like her mother, only nicer.

Paige raised sad eyes. "I get so discouraged. I tell her the same things over and over again and she doesn't remember. One minute she's fine and the next she asks how long it is until Valentine's Day."

"She needs time." He gave her shoulders a comforting squeeze, hoping it was true. "Considering what she's been through, we're damned lucky she's not a—" he bit off his words before he could say "vegetable" and substituted "—a whole lot worse."

"I know, and I'm grateful. I just can't help but wonder if . . . well, if she'll ever be the same as she was."

They had reached the hospital's front doors and paused for a moment. Ben rested both hands on her shoulders and she gazed up at him with perfect confidence. There was a bond between them, forged of shared hopes and fears, and he believed she drew as much comfort from it as he did.

He grinned coaxingly. "Maybe she won't be the same. Maybe she'll be better. There must have been room for at least a little improvement."

Her rueful smile gave her away. "Maybe just a tiny bit," she conceded.

"In the meantime, go get some rest. You're worn out, little one."

"I'm having dinner with Daddy and Sandra and the boys. That always cheers me up. They've been wonderful through this whole thing, although why. . ."

Her voice trailed off but Ben knew. Juliana hadn't exactly come through for her ex-husband, even if he had for her.

"Good. Then I'll see you tomorrow."

She nodded and her hazel eyes sparkled with mischief. "I don't get it—why are you spending so much time here? The doctors and nurses may believe that wild story about an engagement, but I know better."

Ben shook his head ruefully. "I guess since I'm the one who brought her in, I want to be the one who takes her out again."

She rose on tiptoe and stared earnestly into his eyes. "You're wonderful," she said. "You act tough, but I see right through you. You've been a real friend." She planted a quick, shy kiss on his clean-shaven jaw, smiled and turned away.

Stunned, Ben watched her hurry past the glass doors. Damn, this was getting sticky.

Walking slowly to his pickup, he thought longingly of the little neighborhood bar he passed each time he drove home from this hospital. Maybe just one drink—only he knew it wouldn't be just one.

Alcohol hadn't eased his pain before, and it damn sure couldn't help him now. He knew that, intellectually, but it was so hard to resist the urge to escape both the memories and the reality.

He threw open the unlocked door of his truck and climbed inside. He took a deep breath and sat there for a moment, perfectly still; then he thrust the key into the ignition. He had it under control now. He knew he wouldn't stop at the bar, no matter how much he wanted to.

And he did want to. He really did.

THEY WOULDN'T BRING HER a computer, so she couldn't get any work done. They insisted she eat the horrible food and blow in that crazy plastic tube—to keep from catching pneumonia, they said. But she knew it was so much horse hockey.

"I want to go home," she insisted to everyone who entered her room. "When can I go home?"

"Soon," they all responded. "If you eat everything and follow orders." They made it sound easy. It wasn't.

Embarrassed by her shaved head, she refused to see anyone except Paige and Ben and Stella. Other visitors were duly announced, then sent on their way with excuses. Deeply depressed, horribly confused, Juliana simply didn't care.

On March 27, six weeks after she entered the hospital, she dressed in her own robe and slippers and sat on the edge of the bed, ready for discharge. She held a book in her hands, unread. She found it impossible to concentrate; she would read a paragraph—sometimes just a sentence or a line—and realize minutes later that her mind had wandered somewhere else entirely.

Anything, however inconsequential, disturbed her ability to concentrate. But what now drew her attention was a revelation of major proportions.

Her fingernails looked as if they belonged to the Dragon Lady. Juliana stared at them as if she'd never seen fingernails before—and she hadn't. Not this long, on the tips of her own fingers.

She lifted her left hand, running the pad of her thumb along the edges of her nails. Incredible! She'd always kept her nails short, but not because she preferred them that way; they were so soft that they split and broke. With her active life-style, she simply couldn't get any length.

For six weeks she'd lain in bed doing nothing, so her nails had grown and grown and grown. They were in desperate need of shaping, but to her, they were positively beautiful.

She heard footsteps and looked up, ready to share this exciting news with Paige. Instead, Ben appeared in the doorway, his broad shoulders nearly filling it.

"Oh," she said, disappointed. "It's you."

His mouth set in a sardonic curve. "Very well, thank you. Nice of you to ask. And you?"

He walked inside, followed by Dr. Crow. The doctor held a chart, which he flipped open. He glanced at a few pages and closed the cover again. He grinned at Juliana. "Ready to go, I see."

"I've been ready," she said in a surly tone. Despite the fact that she'd been eager to leave, now that the day had come she felt perversely frightened and unprepared.

Ben moved to the far side of the bed, swinging a shopping bag in one fist. "Any last-minute instructions, Doc?"

"Not many." Dr. Crow crossed to Juliana and picked up her wrist. As he spoke, his fingers probed for her pulse. "No medication, no restrictions beyond those of good sense. You can do just about anything you feel like doing. Get plenty of rest, eat good meals. I want to see you a week from today."

The two men looked at her expectantly and she looked out the window.

"Any questions?" Dr. Crow asked finally.

Yes! Am I all right? Have I lost my mind? Half my mind? A quarter? How long does it take hair to grow back? If I get mad and scream my head off will this happen to me again?

"Any questions?" he repeated.

"No," she mumbled. "None."

"In that case, take care. I'll see you in a week. And if you have any problems, any questions, call, okay?"

Juliana nodded. When he left the room she felt abandoned.

Ben touched her arm. "I'll start loading up all this greenery. Then I'll come back for you."

Her eyes widened and she drew an outraged breath. "Where's Paige? *She's* the one who's supposed to take me home."

"Juliana . . ."

She wouldn't be soothed. *"Where's my daughter?"*

"I told her to go on to class and I'd—"

"You had no right! I'm her *mother!*" She clenched her hands into fists. Her newly discovered fingernails bit into her palms and she hastily unclenched her hands.

Ben's face darkened and he leaned toward her. Instinctively she drew back.

He cupped her chin with one hand and forced her to meet his angry gaze. "You've been running that girl ragged. Bitch, bitch, bitch, that's all she's heard out of you."

"But—" Tears sprang in her eyes. The big bully. She hadn't the strength to pull away from him.

He went on relentlessly. "I know you've been sick. I know you're frightened and confused. But it's time you realized that whatever you went through, *she* went through something just as bad in its own way."

All her emotions seemed to lie just beneath the surface. His words conjured up an image of Paige as something akin to the Poor Little Match Girl. "I—I'm sorry." She could barely get the words out.

"Well, hell." He sounded disgusted. For a moment more their glances held, but he no longer looked angry. He slid his hand from her chin down to her throat, his touch light and nonthreatening. "I'm sorry, too. Paige is a great girl...woman...person...whatever. You've done a hell of a job with her, but now you've got to lighten up."

Juliana sniffled, acutely surprised by the comfort to be found in human contact. His fingers felt warm and reassuring on her throat, and he was saying wonderful, true things about her daughter. "Okay," she managed.

"Then why are you crying?" He sounded perplexed. He dropped his hand and stepped away from the bed.

"Because I can't leave here looking like this!" She lifted her hands to her cropped head. Tears streamed down her face in earnest.

He gave an impatient snort. "I know that." He opened the shopping bag and whipped out a black knit stocking cap. With a flourish, he placed it on her head and pulled it clear down over her ears.

He nodded with satisfaction. "There, you look great. Happy now?"

She lifted her hands and clutched the cap on either side, the heels of her palms meeting beneath her chin. His grin was infectious and she returned it reluctantly. "Happy may not be the word I'm searching for—and I'm searching a lot these days. Will you settle for 'resigned'?"

He gave her a thumbs-up gesture and turned to pick up an arrangement of flowers.

"Leave them," Juliana decided suddenly. "The nurses can give them to sick people. I just want out of here."

"You got it. I'll whistle up a wheelchair and we're gone."

She watched his powerful figure stride into the hall. Sighing, she looked around the room one last time.

Her life had changed irrevocably here. More had happened to her than getting shorter hair and longer fingernails.

And as soon as she could think straight, she'd figure out what the hell it was.

JULIANA AND PAIGE shared a sprawling house in the best residential area of Summerhill. They'd lived there for two years, longer than they usually stayed in one place. Juliana had bought the house because it was a good investment just as she'd bought the other seven houses they'd lived in since the divorce.

Thus when Ben carried her through the front door, he saw nothing inside that bore her imprint. Professionally decorated in blue and cream, the house was a testament to educated taste, a healthy bank account and nothing else.

He deposited her on the cream-colored couch and propped pillows behind her back and head. "That wasn't so bad, was it?"

She gave him a wan smile. She'd hardly spoken on the ride from the hospital. "Piece of cake." She sounded tired.

The stocking cap slipped off and fell to the carpet beside her. She didn't seem to notice so he left it there. He didn't find her super-short hair a big deal, now that he was past the initial shock. It was already growing back and it looked as soft and silky as a baby's.

"I'll bring in the rest of your stuff." He started for the door, but her voice stopped him.

"Would you mind handing me the telephone first? There's a—" She groped for the word. Finally she burst out, "You know, one of those without wires?" Her frown screamed at him, "*Help me!*"

"Cordless phone."

She sighed with relief. "A *cordless* phone in the kitchen, through there." She pointed.

He wanted to tell her no, he wouldn't bring it to her. In his opinion, she needed rest, not a telephone. But she'd looked so scared when she couldn't think of the word that he didn't have the heart to throw her any curves.

So he brought her the telephone and set about emptying the Mercedes. He hadn't wanted to drive it to pick her up, but Paige had pointed out the obvious, that it would be more comfortable than his pickup. Juliana hadn't even seemed to notice he was driving her wheels as if he owned them. He didn't think she'd have noticed if he'd picked her up in a tank.

He piled the few things from the hospital in the front hall and walked back into the living room. She lay as he had left her, clutching the telephone. She stared straight ahead, her eyes wide but unfocused. He was sure she hadn't moved a muscle since he put the phone in her hand, not even to dial.

He felt an unwelcome surge of sympathy and ruthlessly tamped it down. He needed to keep his distance, damn it. He said brusquely, "I'll fix you a cup of tea and then I'm outta here."

She started as if she'd forgotten he was even in the house. "You're not going to leave me alone!"

He glanced at his wristwatch. "Paige'll be here within thirty minutes. You want a baby-sitter?"

That stiffened her spine. "No, and I don't want a cup of tea, either. If you're in such a hurry, go."

"I'm used to your temper tantrums so I'll ignore that. You'll take the tea and like it." He turned toward the kitchen, but not before he caught a glimpse of her crestfallen expression. "Want a sandwich or something with it?"

"No!"

"Not even a loaf of bread or a jug of wine?" He already regretted speaking to her so sharply, but it was for her own good. *She has to get used to not having me at her beck and call*, he thought almost desperately. *She's not an invalid and I won't encourage her to act like one.*

". . . a book of verse—and thou beside me singing in the wilderness." She seemed to have completely forgotten her displeasure. Quick excitement sparkled in her eyes. "Omar Khayyam I remember, but I forget . . . what the hell kind of telephone? Detached?"

He chuckled. "Cordless. *Cordless*. But if you had Miss Patch for English, I'm not surprised. She had a real thing for old Omar."

"Yes, yes." She looked feverishly intent. "And Mr. Hugo for biology and Mrs. Blanchard for math and..."

Ben nodded, sensing that she needed to test her memory and command of the language for some reason he didn't fully understand. He sat down beside her on the sofa, pressing her bent legs aside to make room. His hip settled comfortably against hers and he looped his left arm over her knees.

She laid the telephone on the coffee table and shifted to make room for him. "And Mr. Gonzalez. Did you have Mr. Gonzalez for Spanish?"

"Nope. I took French. *Parlez-vous Français?*"

She laughed. "No, and neither do you if you took French at Summerhill High School."

"*Tout de suite*. Does that mean 'right on'?"

Her expression brimmed with almost manic gaiety. She reached up and took his hand, the one dangling in front of her thighs as he leaned against her. She seemed to be practically begging his forgiveness. "Thanks for humoring me."

"Moi?" He tried to disentangle his fingers, but she hung on. Something about the way she looked at him, the way her fingers curled around his, made the hair on the back of his neck prickle in warning. Her lips looked soft, soft and inviting, now that she was eager and smiling instead of raising hell. He wondered how it would feel to curve his hands over the beautiful shape of her head and—*Judas Priest! She's barely out of the hospital. What the hell's the matter with me?*

He stiffened, but she didn't seem to notice. "My memory seems a little...uncertain. Paige said I asked her the same questions over and over again, and I suppose I did the same with you."

He licked his lips and tried to concentrate on her words, tried to ignore the growing tightness in his chest. "Hey, who's counting? The doc said to expect a few little glitches in your memory computer. Just be glad your lease didn't expire prematurely. That's a little real-estate humor."

She groaned and clutched her stomach as if in pain. The moment of anxiety passed for him; he drew a steadying breath and relaxed.

She rolled her eyes. "A little humor is right—very little."

So he'd imagined it—whatever the hell had just happened. What a jerk.

The doorbell pealed. She jumped and her eyes opened wide. "I don't want to see anyone," she said in a breathless rush. "Don't let anybody in—please! I can't let anyone see me until . . . until I can . . ."

He realized she didn't know how to finish her thought—until when? Until her hair grew back? That would take months. Until she had regained all her strength, both mental and physical?

He stood up. "You can't hide forever," he said, speaking bluntly because she'd just given him an uncomfortable moment. The fact that she didn't know it cut no ice with him at all. He'd felt things he hadn't felt in a hell of a long time and it was her fault.

She stared at him, her expression one of shock.

He was relentless. "You've never been a coward. Don't start now."

"I'm not! It's just that . . ."

He could see her struggle. The old poker face was gone and her every thought and emotion seemed nakedly exposed. *Jeez*, he thought, maybe she's right. Maybe she should be careful who she saw until she got everything under control.

Maybe the last person on earth she needs to see is me.

She took a deep breath and relaxed back onto the cushions. "All right, damn you. Answer the door."

She didn't smile, but he didn't care. At least she wasn't cowering and begging for mercy.

JULIANA HEARD the voices at the door.

"Boss lady here?"

"Sure, Stella, come on in."

Stella sailed into the living room, Ben moving on through to the kitchen.

"He always was a good kid." Stella grinned after him. "Lillian positively doted on her baby brother, and if truth be told, so did I."

She turned toward Juliana. "How's the boss?" Stella laid an armload of files on the coffee table and placed a briefcase on the floor. She pulled up a chair and sat down.

"Okay, I guess. How's everything at the office?" Even as she uttered the words, Juliana realized she didn't much care. No, that wasn't true. She cared, but she didn't feel ready to face it.

"Not the mess you'd imagine, given how long you've been away." Stella picked up the top file. "I don't want you to think we're getting along fine without you because we're not, but the roof hasn't fallen in or anything. Everyone's pitched in—they all send their best and want to know when they can come see you."

Juliana tried to keep the anxiety she felt out of her voice. "Not for a while. I . . . I'm just not up to it yet."

Stella's expression softened. "Honey, if it's your hair—"

Juliana yanked her hand away from her head; she hadn't even realized she was running one palm over the stubble.

Stella leaned forward and patted Juliana's cheek. "If it bothers you, why not get a wig?"

"That's so phony."

"Then tie a pretty scarf around your ears and it'll look like you planned it."

Juliana laughed ruefully. "How long do you think it'll take to grow out?"

Stella considered. "Long enough to get a cut with some style in it, I'd say... oh, six months or so."

"Six months!" Juliana groaned. "I can't wait six months to go out in public."

"It won't take you six months to do that." Stella spoke confidently. "It's just a matter of getting used to it, Juli. After a while you won't give it a thought."

"Don't think so, huh?" Juliana gave her friend and secretary a doubtful glance. "You're talking with a lot of authority, here. Do you know something I don't?"

Stella sighed. "Do you remember my sister, Irene?"

"The one who lives in Tulsa?"

"That's right. About five years ago when Irene was sick and I went back there—remember?—she had a brain aneurysm."

Juliana was aghast at her own insensitivity. "I guess at the time it just didn't mean anything to me. I mean, I was sorry it was your sister, but I didn't understand what the problem was."

"There was no reason you should." Stella picked up a file. "Let's plow through these papers so you can get some rest."

"But how is Irene?" Juliana, crushed by her faux pas, tried to redeem herself.

"Fine." Stella softened the brusque word with a quick smile. "Now if we can just get started...."

It was tough, trying to concentrate on what Stella was saying. When she would pause for directions or for a simple yes or no, Juliana would hesitate, then force herself to respond. But all she could bring herself to utter were inane things. "Whatever you think... Ask John to look this over... Sounds good to me."

Soon Stella closed the briefcase and smiled. "That should do it for the moment. I'm really sorry I barged in, but we needed guidance."

Juliana tried not to let her disbelief show. She doubted she'd been any real help at all. Before she could say so, Ben entered, carrying a cup.

"Coffee, tea or... something else?" he asked Stella, wiggling his eyebrows and setting the cup with its trailing tea bag tag on the coffee table.

"I'm tempted, but no, thanks. Gotta run." She picked up the briefcase and the files and smiled at Juliana. "Anything I can do for you, hon?"

"One thing." Juliana took a deep breath. "Cary Goddard—he must know what happened to me, since I didn't keep our date for the Valentine Ball, right?"

Stella and Ben exchanged guarded glances. Juliana wanted to scream in frustration.

"Mr. Goddard knows," Stella said, turning away.

"Wait a minute." Juliana's frown took in both of them and she began to tap an anxious rhythm on the coffee table with the fingers of one hand. "Who spoke to him?"

The silence stretched on and on. Then Ben shrugged.

"You did," he said.

4

"I DON'T BELIEVE YOU! I haven't seen Cary Goddard since—" Juliana's eyes widened; she obviously didn't know how to finish her sentence.

Ben hated feeling sorry for her. "Take it easy," he ordered gruffly. "It was the first or second day you were out of intensive care. I got to the hospital just as Goddard was leaving. We . . . spoke briefly in the corridor."

True, Ben had "briefly" offered to rearrange Goddard's face if he showed it outside Juliana's door again. Such a warning probably hadn't been necessary; the guy'd looked green and offered no argument.

Juliana groaned. "Was my head still bandaged or did he see me . . . this way?" She rolled her eyes up, indicating her nearly naked scalp.

"You're really shallow enough to care?" Ben shot back.

"I saw Mr. Goddard at the office," Stella volunteered. "He said he'd be in touch." She hesitated. "He hasn't."

Juliana groaned. Stella gave Ben a concerned glance. He gestured toward the door with a slight movement of his chin and she took the hint and left.

Ben leaned against the back of the chair she'd vacated. "Anything else before I split?"

"I want a cigarette."

"No chance."

"I'm not joking—I want a cigarette. Who are you, my mother?"

"No, and I'm not your daughter or your ex-husband or anybody else you're used to pushing around."

He glared at her and she glared back, until her lips began to tremble. He relented, but only slightly. "You don't really want a cigarette," he said cajolingly.

"Well, I want *something*!" She closed her eyes for a moment, then looked straight into his face. "You play dirty."

"I play to win. How do you play?"

"Currently, with half a deck." Her smile looked only partly forced. "I just want things to be the way they were."

"You sure?" He was egging her on and he knew it. "Your life was perfect, then. No room for improvement."

She lifted her chin, her long-lashed hazel eyes stormy. "I never claimed to be perfect," she shot back at him.

"Sure you did. All the way through high school."

"I hope you're joking." Color flooded her face. "I wouldn't put money on it, though. You never did like me very much."

"No, not much."

"At least you're brutally honest." She glared at him.

"If it's any consolation, I like you a little better now than I did then." He said it reluctantly.

"Well, whoopty-do," she scoffed. "I guess that's what they call damning with faint praise. What changed your mind?"

He'd wondered himself and finally came to a conclusion. "Sharing adversity. I've seen you with your hair down, so to speak."

She gasped and lifted both hands to her head. "You've seen me with my hair *gone*. A nice person wouldn't rub it in."

"I never claimed to be nice."

She pursed her lips disapprovingly while he tried to keep his face as blank as an unsullied page. She looked thoroughly disgruntled. "I'm not perfect and you're not nice. We make a great pair."

He thrust his hands into his jean pockets and rocked back on his heels. He had no intention of being half of anybody's pair. "Pair of what?"

"Pair of jerks," she threw back at him.

He shrugged and turned away.

"Give me a break," she called after him. "I *am* going to be a better person. Everything's going to be different now. You might even learn to like me."

"Riiiight." He kept on walking. "I'll hold my breath."

PAIGE PULLED INTO the driveway as Ben walked to his pickup. She jumped out of her car and ran up to clutch at his arm.

"Is Mother inside? How'd it go?"

He shrugged. "Not too bad." He stopped at the driver's side of the truck and leaned against the door. "She's making progress. It's slow, but it's progress."

Paige sighed. "I know. I try to be patient, but I'm not very good at it."

"Better than *she* is."

Paige laughed, as Ben had intended, but she seemed distracted. He tilted her chin with gentle fingers and gazed down at her quizzically. She wouldn't look at him; her eyelids drooped, concealing her expression. "Okay," he said. "Let's have it. What's on your mind?"

She drew in a slow breath, then expelled it in a rush. "I'm going to work at the hospital. As a volunteer, I mean."

"What brought that on, as if I need to ask?"

She darted him an anxious-looking smile. "You know. I . . . I can't tell you what it meant to me, to see what they did for Mother. It was like magic, Ben." Her big hazel eyes widened even more. "She was as good as dead and they *saved* her, they brought her back. I'll never be able to repay them for what they did except by... by..."

Her furtive glance told him what was coming. "By joining them."

"Yes." She hung her head, the shining fall of brown hair obscuring her expression.

Ben frowned, puzzling over her nervousness. Did she think her mother would object to a little grateful do-gooding? But what if it were more? "We're not simply talking volunteering here, are we? We're talking career change."

She said nothing, just stared guiltily at the ground.

"Paige?"

Slowly she raised her face. "Yes," she whispered, her expression terribly vulnerable. "I want to help people, the way my mother was helped. I suppose that sounds really dumb and naive but... but... I never wanted to be a business major anyway!"

Ben blinked at the passion in her voice. "Then why are you?"

She wrung her hands together, her soft lips trembling. "I had to declare a major and I couldn't think of anything better. She was always after me about it so I just did it to get her off my back."

Ben groaned. "You plan to tell her right away?"

Paige took a step backward, one hand flying to her throat. "Good grief, no! Not until she's recovered—and in a good mood. A *really* good mood."

"Do moods get that good?" Ben muttered.

"What?"

"I think it's a good idea to wait awhile. You may change your mind after you see what nursing is really like."

"Maybe."

She obviously didn't think so. He knew when he was being humored.

She grinned. "I feel better already, having you to talk to." Without apparent self-consciousness, she wrapped her arms around his waist in an enthusiastic hug.

He kept his own arms stiff at his sides. "Just take it slow and everything will be fine." He didn't want to commit further than that but heard himself adding, "if you need me, you know where to find me." He gave her shoulders a last light squeeze and set her aside to open the truck door.

"Thanks, Ben."

"It was nothing, kiddo."

"It was everything. I couldn't have survived this without you."

He settled himself on the seat and closed the truck door. "Sure you could. You're your mother's daughter, which means you can survive anything."

He winked and started the engine; it caught with a whine followed by a snarl.

She blew him a kiss and stepped back. He read her lips as he turned the vehicle out of the curved driveway: "Thank you."

Glowering out at the brilliant spring day, he guided the pickup toward Buena Suerte Canyon. Somehow he didn't feel he'd managed to untangle himself from the Robinson women.

Worse, it didn't seem like he'd really tried all that hard.

JULIANA STOOD stark naked in front of the mirrored wall of her bathroom, staring at her reflection. It was her second day home and her first chance to take inventory.

What she saw dismayed her. She looked thin and gaunt, her ribs sharp ridges beneath her skin. Shadows lay like purple smudges beneath her eyes and hollowed out her cheekbones. She trailed trembling fingers across her cheek, letting the long fingernails drag lightly across skin flaccid and lacking in tone.

You can never be too thin or too rich. She'd said that recently to someone, but to whom or upon what occasion she had no idea. Gritting her teeth, she ignored the weakness that grew and spread through her limbs with each passing second. She needed to know it all.

A slightly puckered scar began three inches above her navel and rose for another three inches, neatly bisecting her stomach with its purply pink path. It didn't hurt. She didn't even know its origin until Paige explained about the second operation.

"They put in a shunt, Mama, a tube from your head to your stomach to drain...stuff, you know, fluids. But you didn't get better so they did a third operation to take it out."

Juliana raised her right hand, so accustomed to the yellowing bruises on her arm that she didn't really see them anymore. With her forefinger, she lightly traced a small vertical scar directly behind her ear. About an inch long, it lay right at the hairline. She knew, without comprehending the source of her knowledge, that this was part of the shunt procedure that hadn't worked.

Oh, it was all so confusing!

She had another small scar, so small in fact that she didn't know how she'd come to find it. Less than two inches long, it was on her groin, and a nurse had explained at some dim and misty point that it was the result of an angiogram.

"A narrow tube—a catheter—was inserted in an artery in your groin and threaded up to your brain . . . the doctor injected a dye which shows up on an X ray and then he watched on an X-ray screen while the dye traveled—"

"*Through my brain?*"

Juliana shuddered and closed her eyes briefly, steeling herself to go on. It all seemed such a horrible intrusion. She swallowed hard and reached for a hand mirror on the blue-tiled countertop.

Try as she might, she couldn't see where they had actually opened her skull. She could feel the spot with her fingers, on the right side of her head, two inches directly above her ear . . . a faint indentation, a comfortable fit for the pads of two fingers, maybe three. It felt to her much like the soft spot on an infant's head.

At first she hadn't been able to bring herself to touch the spot, but touch was the only sense with which she could define it. She couldn't see anything; even what little hair she had got in the way, as did her inability to move her neck easily and freely from side to side.

And her eyes . . . she had a new and unexpected difficulty in focusing for more than a few seconds. Much the same as the difficulty she had concentrating . . . she wondered if those two problems could be related.

Or maybe she didn't really want to see that last, worst evidence. Her hair was growing back; why borrow trouble?

Trembling with strain, she pulled on a sweat suit and joined Paige in the family room. A fresh pot of blueberry tea and a plate of oat bran muffins rested on an end table. Tired and a little depressed, Juliana settled back against the tumble of cushions on the couch.

As Paige finished pouring the tea, the telephone rang. She answered in the kitchen, appearing moments later with the remote receiver in her hands.

"It's John at your office," she said, covering the mouthpiece with one hand. "He says he hopes he's not disturbing you and he hopes you're feeling better."

"Yes, sure, I'm fine."

"And he says Stella's out of the office and he needs to put some checks into the safe. He wants to know if that's okay and if you'll give him the combination."

"Tell him fine," Juliana said automatically, then realized she had no idea what the combination might be: she couldn't even remember the first number. In fact, at that moment, she didn't remember the location of the safe itself.

"On second thought, tell him to just hang on to the stuff until Stella gets back."

"Okay." Paige walked out of the room, talking into the receiver as she went.

Juliana lay back in a cold sweat, racking her brain to remember the combination to the safe. Or the address of her office. Or her own telephone number.

Or her daughter's birthday.

JULIANA SAW her doctor one week after discharge, but the visit made little impression on her and within a few hours she'd all but forgotten it. She didn't remember what he had said to her or what she had said to him. All she knew was that he hadn't done any of those scary procedures she'd dreaded.

Nor had she brought up any of the multitude of minor confusions with which she struggled daily. Somehow it seemed that to do so would lend them credibility and substance. Better to simply wait and see, even though she had never felt so fragmented and unsure. Stimuli of all kinds slid off her memory like an egg off new Teflon.

Even Stella's reports on office happenings failed to make an impression on Juliana. Everything seemed to be progressing smoothly, which didn't exactly please her on the one hand, but on the other, made it possible to delay her return.

Stella concluded each conversation with a question. "So when are you coming back to work, Juliana?"

Juliana would put her off. "Soon. Just as soon as the doctor gives the word."

In truth, she didn't intend to go back until she could return exactly as she'd left—mentally as well as physically. And the way things were going... *I'd kill for a cigarette*, she thought suddenly. *To hell with the office—I want a smoke.*

What had happened to the carton of cigarettes she'd stashed in her lingerie chest just a few days before she...what? Got sick? Got hurt? Fell over like some fool? She'd never figured out what to call what had happened to her, which added to her irritation.

Furiously she pulled out the narrow drawers, dumping them on the floor before tossing them aside. There were no cigarettes in any of them.

"Damn!" She stood there, swaying on her feet and breathing hard, tears backing up into a lump in her throat.

From the other side of the bedroom door, Paige called. "Mama, you have company."

The dark cloud of Juliana's despondency shifted slightly. "Ben?"

"Yes, and—"

The rest was muffled as Juliana hurried across the room, threw open the door and brushed past.

She had missed Ben more than she'd realized.

"Mama, slow down and let me tell you—"

Too late. Juliana greeted Ben with a broad smile which slipped at sight of the woman beside him.

Ben's guarded expression never changed. "Look who I found just about to ring your doorbell."

Barbara Snell stepped forward with a solicitous smile. Despite fifty years on Planet Earth, Barbara still managed to project an impression of charmingly helpless confusion.

Which, Juliana knew to her sorrow, covered a mind like a computer. For the past three years, she and Barbara had vied for the coveted Real Estate Star honor given annually by the Summerhill Real Estate Board. The winner received a tiny gold star-shaped pin with a diamond chip for each succeeding award.

Barbara stood there now with a three-chip pin; Juliana didn't even have the pin—forget the chips! She gritted her teeth. *And this was my year, damn it!*

"Juliana!"

"Barbara!"

And a rough-voiced aside: "Jesus!"

The women embraced cautiously and Juliana glared at Ben over Barbara's shoulder. He shrugged and rolled his eyes.

"Juliana, you look wonderful," Barbara declared in her soft, little-girl voice. "You're not nearly as thin and frail as I expected. And you look cute with short hair!"

Juliana clenched her hands together at her sides and refused to cower or try to cover her head with her hands, as she longed to do. To her way of thinking, her head resembled a briar patch, and under no circumstances could it be called cute. The rest of her wasn't in such hot shape, either.

But then, she wondered, what the hell could anyone say? "You look like ten miles of bad road?"

Ben and Paige left the room. He'd been helping her with a math class, Juliana knew. She watched them go with envy. They'd gotten close during the days spent together at the hospital, and even closer now that they were spending all that time over the books. She wasn't entirely sure she approved.

Barbara sighed. "That's a nice piece of land Ben owns out there in Buena Suerte Canyon."

Juliana thought the sigh was for the man as much as the land. "Yes."

Barbara looked like a teenaged girl contemplating a hot fudge sundae she knew she'd regret. "I suppose now you'll have an inside track with him."

Juliana frowned. "What are you talking about?"

"You know. After what the two of you have been through together, he's sure to sell to Cary Goddard. That'll bring you a nice piece of change."

Aghast, Juliana stared at the other woman. "Wait a minute, wait a minute. How do you know what we've 'been through together,' as you put it?"

Barbara laughed patronizingly. "Oh, Juliana, everybody knows you collapsed at his place, and that he took you to the hospital. Why my goodness, he practically lived there. He wouldn't let *anybody* in to see you—you'd think he was your husband, the way he acted."

"And you're suggesting that now I'm in a position to talk Ben into selling? You must think I'm a real—"

"Businesswoman!" Barbara winked. "Hey, far be it from me to criticize. Business is business, but that's not why I came. I just wanted to see for myself how you're getting along. Everybody sends their regards."

Juliana refused to squirm. She was convinced Barbara's only motive was morbid curiosity but didn't entirely blame her. Who wouldn't be curious? "As you can see, I'll soon be good as new."

Barbara raised her brows ingenuously and her glance flicked over the shorn scalp. "Absolutely. If this hadn't happened, I truly believe you'd have given me a real run for the money for the Star award this year." Ostentatiously she fingered the gold pin, the one with the three diamond chips.

"How sweet of you to say so, Babs. I think so, too. How have you been doing in my absence?" It hurt Juliana's face to keep smiling.

Barbara looked as satisfied as a cat with a mouthful of mouse. "Very *very* well. But you know, Juliana, nobody's nailed down the Good Samaritan award at this point. Maybe that's the one you ought to go for."

Yes, and you should— "Do you think so?"

Barbara's baby-blue eyes widened. "Of course. I mean, your father won it so many times they *gave* it to him and bought a new perpetual trophy. Like father, like daughter."

The old, familiar feeling of frustration welled up in Juliana's chest. It seemed her father would forever be held up as a measure of her own shortcomings.

Nobody seemed to care that she'd taken her father's failing business and turned it into one of the most successful real-estate firms in town. All anybody remembered was that Webster Malone was the man who'd find a way to make good things happen for others.

At the expense of himself, of his wife, of his daughter... She was spared a response by the timely return of Ben and Paige.

Barbara jumped to her feet. "Ben, I've got a couple of clients who are interested in learning more about home security. I heard you've been doing a little consulting."

"Sure." Ben looked past her to where Juliana sat.

Juliana examined him from beneath lowered lashes. He looked damned good, powerful and sure of himself in denim and chambray. She felt an unexpected prickle of awareness. It threw her off balance and she made the mistake of looking up. His deep blue gaze connected with hers. For a heady moment their glances locked. But something disturbed her. There was something different about him... She frowned.

Of course! He was clean-shaven! The day he'd taken her to the hospital, he'd had a days-old beard...but while she was in the hospital he...had he shaved then or...why did she notice this now? In her annoyance, she closed her eyes and shook her head impatiently.

Ben's harsh voice drew her back. "Okay," he snapped, his face hardening. "Forget I mentioned it, Juliana. You ready, Barbara?"

Barbara smiled her goodbyes and followed Ben from the room, her eagerness apparent.

Paige turned on her mother the instant they were alone. "Why were you so rude to him? He was only asking—"

"What are you talking about?" He hadn't asked a thing—had he?

"Just now. It was nice of him to offer to take you out to his place for a change of scene. I'd have thought you'd jump at the chance, and you don't even give him the courtesy of an answer. You just shake your head like he was some kid trying to sell you cookies or something."

Paige stood stiffly in the doorway, her soft mouth set in a disapproving line. "Just don't hold your breath until you get another invitation from him," she said wrathfully, and stomped out of the room.

BEN HEARD HIS TELEPHONE ringing as he walked across the yard. He'd just left Juliana's and he wasn't in the best of moods. Without any particular interest or curiosity, he banged open the kitchen door and stepped inside.

The jangle of the bell continued. He grabbed the receiver off the wall-mounted telephone and issued a terse greeting.

A long silence . . . someone playing games, he thought, preparing to hang up. Then he heard Julianna's voice. "Ben? It's me, Juliana."

"Juliana who?"

"Very funny. I . . . I called to apologize."

Beware of Greeks bearing gifts—or real estate people bearing apologies. He kept his voice noncommittal. "That right?"

"Yes. Paige really chewed me out after you left. But the fact is, I didn't even hear what you said to me. I . . . I guess I zoned out there for a minute. Will you forgive me?"

He hesitated. "Sure," he said finally, not meaning it. He added a half-hearted "Why not?"

He knew why not. He'd been responding to temptation when he'd blurted out his invitation. Hell, he'd come to his senses the instant the words left his mouth.

She pressed on. "Good. Then it's all right if I come visit you one of these days?"

"Want to keep your eye on the place for your client, I suppose."

He heard her suck in her breath. "I'm not like that, Ben."

He took a few seconds to steady himself. "No," he said at last. "I don't suppose you are."

"Thank you for admitting that," she said, and hung up the telephone.

He stood for a while, leaning against the kitchen counter and staring moodily out the window.

She was getting to him, despite everything he could do to prevent it. He hadn't had time to erect his usual defenses. Her fight for survival had become very personal to him, and now that the crisis was past he found himself toting around all kinds of excess emotional baggage.

Somehow her recovery had come to symbolize his resurrection as a worthwhile member of the human race.

He'd come back to Summerhill convinced on an abstract level that his only chance to regain his self-respect lay in hanging on to this land and making it work. But now he wondered if that would be enough.

Through the long days and nights of Juliana's ordeal, he had come to realize how much he needed to care on a personal level. At first it had been Paige who cracked his defenses. Now Juliana was widening that crack to a canyon.

I've been alone with these damned avocado trees too long, he told himself. He shook away thoughts of her and walked to the refrigerator. But again he hesitated, leaning his forehead against the cool white exterior. He closed his eyes.

This situation with Juliana was about to get out of hand. His nerves still tingled with the aftereffects of that once-over she'd given him. Did she realize what was going on? Somehow he doubted it. She hadn't been catching many subtleties lately.

Gradually he became aware of meowing and scratching sounds at the door. It was that damned stray cat again. *If it hangs around here it'll starve to death 'cause I sure as hell won't feed it*, he thought wrathfully.

He opened the refrigerator and pulled out a half-full carton of milk. He opened the flap and took a swig from the container.

Outside the door, the cat meowed pitifully.

Of course, cats could be useful when you lived in the country. Good way to fight those avocado-eating mice and rats without resorting to dangerous poisons. On the other hand, domestic animals in this country—dogs as well as cats—usually wound up bait for the coyotes.

Ben walked to the screen door. Moodily he lifted the milk carton to his lips and drank. He kicked open the screen and glared down at the scrawny little black-and-orange feline.

It was beyond a doubt the ugliest animal he'd ever seen with its matted fur and crazy calico hide. Somebody probably tied it in a sack and dumped it off in the canyon because it was too ugly to live, Ben theorized. *Move on, cat. I got nothin' to give to nobody.*

The creature turned its pointy whiskered face toward him, its sharp little kitten teeth bared in a piteous yowl.

Well, hell. He knelt and drew a disgusted breath, considering the creature. "Okay, cat," he announced, "here's the deal."

He leaned over and picked up a foil pan he'd put out earlier in the week with bread crumbs for the birds. He began to pour milk into the pan. The kitten managed to get beneath the flow and Ben cursed as the white liquid flattened the animal's wild pelt.

"If you're gonna hang around here, you'll have to earn your keep, you little freeloader," he said to the ecstatic kitten, who lapped frantically at the milk. "I won't have any damned animals in the house, but you can bunk in the barn if you keep the mice out. Got that? I see a rodent and you're on your way to cat heaven."

The kitten purred with such vigor that its skinny sides vibrated. It lifted its wet head and licked its whiskers as if agreeing to the deal Ben offered.

"Jeez." He stood up. "A damned freeloading cat. Just don't go thinking this means we're friends."

He didn't want any friends. And he sure as hell didn't want any lovers. All he wanted was to be left alone in peace to grow his damned avocados.

JULIANA SAT in Dr. Crow's office, six weeks after her dismissal from the hospital. She'd just had a CAT scan and was waiting to hear the doctor's evaluation.

Carefully she glossed over details that might cast any but the most favorable light on her progress. Why she felt such a desire to excel she didn't know—just her basic competitive nature, she supposed. But whatever anyone else had ever done toward a speedy and complete recovery, she would do better and faster.

The CAT scan had brought a satisfied expression to the doctor's face. Now he leaned back in his chair and nodded. "Juliana, you're a miracle," he said.

Her determined good cheer faltered. "That's not the kind of talk I like to hear from my brain surgeon," she protested.

The doctor laughed. "Sorry, but I can't take all the credit for this one," he admitted. "Sometimes you just gotta figure somebody up there really *does* like you." He rolled his eyes toward the ceiling as if seeking heavenly corroboration.

"Oooookay." She swallowed hard. "I guess that leaves me with just one question."

"And that is?"

She spoke through tight lips. "What are the chances this will happen to me again?"

"Slim and none," he responded promptly. "You're less likely to suffer a second aneurysm than I am the first. Or anyone else who's never had one."

She had been holding her breath; she let it out slowly. "I wouldn't want to go through that again."

"That's not something you need to worry about."

She stood up, light-headed with relief. "Sounds like you're telling me to quit worrying and get on with my life."

The doctor walked around the desk and gave her a quick hug. "That's about it. And to answer the question you're not asking, yes—it's perfectly okay for you to go ahead and marry the guy."

5

"BUT HE TOLD THE DOCTOR we're *engaged*!" Juliana twisted on the car seat to appeal to Stella. "Why on earth would Ben tell such a lie?"

Stella maneuvered her sedan out of the hospital parking lot. "Desperation, mainly."

"Huh?" Juliana frowned. The doctor's unknowing revelation had completely thrown her. She wavered between outrage and a kind of horrified delight. "What's that supposed to mean?"

Stella moved into the flow of traffic before answering. "He thought they wouldn't let him in to see you. He thought—and rightly so—that they wouldn't give him reports on your condition or let him participate in discussions about your prognosis."

"Oh." Juliana slumped back against the seat cushion. After a while she said, "Well, why did he want to? I'm nothing to him."

"You're a human being. That's enough for some people."

Was that all? The possibility didn't please her, although she hadn't consciously assigned any other motive to him. *Engaged to Ben.* The concept sent a prickle of guilty excitement up her spine.

They drove for a while in silence and then Stella asked, "Did he say when you can come back to work?"

"Who?"

"The doctor, of course."

"Oh. Him." Juliana absently ran the fingers of one hand up the nape of her neck, beneath the scarf. Her hair was long enough that it no longer felt like a short-bristled scrub brush to her.

But return to work? *It's too soon! I've only been out of the hospital for six weeks. I'm not ready to go back to work.* There, she admitted to herself. She wasn't ready and had no idea when she would be.

If ever.

So she hedged. "I . . . I'm not sure."

"The longer you wait, the harder it's going to be." Stella turned the car onto Juliana's street.

"I suppose." Juliana hesitated. "Did I tell you the doctor called me a miracle?"

Stella laughed. "Just what you want to hear from your brain surgeon."

"That's what I said. But it kind of got to me."

"What's wrong with being a miracle? Sounds plenty high-toned to me." Stella braked in Juliana's driveway.

"It carries a heavy obligation, that's what's wrong with it. Why did I live when so many others die? What did I ever do to deserve heavenly intervention?"

Stella switched off the ignition and sat quietly for a moment. "Maybe it's not what you've done," she suggested gently. "Maybe it's what you're going to do."

"Just what I need—more pressure." Juliana strove for a light tone. "Stella, do you believe there's a reason for everything?"

"I want to believe it. It's the only thing that makes any sense." Stella smiled suddenly. "But that doesn't necessarily mean you've been saved for some great cosmic purpose, Juliana. I mean, I don't think you have to rush off like Johnny Appleseed and spread seeds of goodness."

Juliana burst out laughing. "That's a relief, anyway."

Stella patted Juliana's hand. "Honey, I don't know if you had a great doctor or divine intervention or a little of both. But I do know you've got one more chance to smell the roses. And if you don't, you're a darned fool."

THE BLAST of the telephone greeted Juliana as she unlocked the front door. She walked into the kitchen as the answering machine kicked in.

"Juliana, it's Barbara. I have some business to discuss with you. I'll take a chance and drop by about four. Hope that's okay. Ta-ta—oh, I almost forgot! Hope you're feeling better. Bye."

Juliana's shoulders slumped. Just what Juliana needed. She sagged onto a stool at the breakfast bar. She should feel elated after receiving a clean bill of health, but the prospect of seeing Barbara was depressing.

Worst of all, the old, familiar craving for nicotine rose in her throat. She wanted—no, *needed*—a cigarette. She hadn't smoked since the day she got . . . since the day it . . . since—

"The hell with it." Digging in her purse, she pulled out her car keys. If Ben was determined to keep her from smoking, he could jolly well lend moral support when she needed it.

She hadn't seen him in a couple of weeks and she hated to think about how much she missed him. He and Paige were in touch. They'd had lunch together just last Saturday but hadn't invited Juliana to join them. She'd been miffed about that.

Yet here she was, pulling to a stop beneath the shade trees next to his pickup truck. For a moment she sat there, clasping the steering wheel, wondering if she really wanted to do this.

I'm only visiting a friend. Why am I making a big deal out of it? she asked herself. She took a deep breath and stepped out of the car.

He was nowhere to be seen. Nervously she patted at the chiffon scarf wrapped and tied around her head, then adjusted the oversized sunglasses perched on her nose. She never went out these days without her "disguise."

She knocked at the kitchen door and called his name. No answer. Frowning, she turned to stare out over the surrounding countryside. All around her the scent of citrus blossoms rose from the canyon floor, a heady perfume she'd never taken time to notice before. *Stop and smell the roses....*

The avocado grove fell away in terraced rows, trees marching along at neatly spaced intervals. Two-thousand-two-hundred avocado trees stood between Cary Goddard and a multi-million-dollar project.

She used to think of this land in terms of the fat commission she'd earn with its sale. Now she simply stood there and wondered why she'd never noticed how beautiful it was. It soothed her soul just to listen to the quiet.

Without thought or plan, she made her way around the right wing of the house. On the far side of the structure, a covered deck supported by concrete posts extended out over the canyon's edge. Juliana climbed up the pebbled steps and walked out onto the fenced wooden platform.

A dilapidated old redwood picnic table stood in the middle of the deck, a matching wooden bench on one side and two old metal lawn chairs on the other. Several redwood planters containing the limp remains of once flourishing plant life rested beside the sliding glass door.

The place wasn't exactly in ruins but Mrs. Ware hadn't had an easy time, keeping it up. She'd obviously grown short of both money and time, after her husband's death, and the shabbiness of the house and outbuildings showed it. And although Ben seemed determined to hang on, country life didn't appear to come naturally to him.

Her eyes lifted to the west. Through a notch in the rolling hills she could see the Pacific Ocean seven or eight miles distant, so beautiful in its frame of blue sky and green fields that it took her breath away.

Footsteps brought her swinging about as Ben rounded the corner of the house. Unexpected pleasure flooded through her at the sight of him, so solid and familiar. She'd missed him. She couldn't deny that any longer.

He reached the steps and tripped. She gasped and started forward, but he didn't fall, just swore under his breath and leaned over to pick something up.

"Damn cat!" But he handled the black and orange kitten gently, scooting it off to one side. The kitten meowed and scampered between his feet again.

"You have a kitten!"

"Not really. I think it's got me."

"It's adorable. What's its name?"

"I call it Freeloader because that's what it is." He nudged the ball of fur aside and the kitten scampered back down the steps and out of sight.

Ben joined her on the edge of the deck. "Nice view, isn't it." His deep voice sounded unusually mellow. He didn't appear in the least surprised to find her prowling around his house.

"Beautiful."

"Won't be quite so nice after the engineers get through with it."

She felt her hackles rise; she knew he enjoyed baiting her. "You have something against engineers?"

"Don't all right-thinking people?" He turned his head to look at her, his expression challenging. "You know what they say—engineers won't be happy until the world's flat and covered with concrete."

She laughed in spite of herself. "There's probably a couple of engineers who'd argue that," she suggested mildly.

"Yeah, but they don't work for Goddard Enterprises."

She opened her mouth to retort, but caught herself in time. *Old habits die hard,* she realized. "I didn't come here to argue the merits of Goddard Enterprises."

Triumphant, she looked at him fully and caught the flash of surprise on his sun-browned face. As his skin darkened from long hours in the grove, the same sun continued to bleach the silky blond hair, leaving random streaks shades lighter. She found the combination of dark skin, pale hair and blue, blue eyes electrifying.

"So what did you come here to argue about, if not Goddard Enterprises?"

It was said teasingly, so she took no offense. "I didn't come to argue at all."

He arched his brows and waited.

She looked away. "I came because . . . I came because I just saw the doctor and I'm feeling . . ."

His glance sharpened. "Nothing's wrong, is it?"

"No." She sighed. It went completely against her grain to let him see her need.

He grunted. "I didn't think so. You look . . ."

She glanced at him quickly, sensing a compliment.

". . . okay."

"Oh."

Ben thought she sounded disappointed. He, on the other hand, felt relief. He'd almost said "terrific," and had caught himself just in time.

When he thought of how she'd looked during those first days and weeks in the hospital, how near death she'd come, her recovery seemed nothing short of a miracle. Before, he'd considered her attractive in a glossy and calculated way. Now he saw in her a new, softer, much more appealing beauty.

The best things about her—intelligence, quick wit, a sense of humor—remained. But he thought her less attractive traits—cynicism, greed, selfishness—were, if not gone entirely, at least held in check.

Minor problems such as too-short hair and an occasional memory lapse seemed a small price to pay for all that improvement. But then, he reminded himself, he wasn't the one doing the paying.

"If you feel okay," he said abruptly, "then what's the matter?"

"Nothing's exactly the matter. I feel sort of . . . pensive. I just didn't want to be alone."

He nodded. He could understand that, although he wished he couldn't. He thrust his thumbs into the pockets of his denims and tried to sound tough. "Yeah, well...I've got a lot of work to do."

"Sure. I understand." Her head drooped.

She looked so dispirited that he felt the damnedest desire to put his arms around her. "Look," he said, disgusted with his inability to hang tough, "I didn't mean—"

"It's okay," she said quickly. She turned toward the steps. "You were working and I interrupted you."

"Don't go."

She looked back quickly, a question in her eyes.

Idiot. "I'm about to tackle the irrigation system, a risky business at best. Sometimes I make it better, sometimes I make it worse." He debated with himself and lost. "If you'd like to tag along . . ."

She grinned, and it was like sunshine after a shower. "I would." She took a step toward him.

His glance connected with hers. Unconsciously he held his breath; after a long moment he shrugged and turned away. He walked down off the deck without looking back. He could hear her following at his heels, and at the moment he didn't know whether that made him happy or not.

THEY WALKED BACK toward the house hours later, from the farthest reaches of the grove, and Juliana realized she hadn't thought of a cigarette since she arrived.

She felt good—tired but satisfied. The beauty of the day surrounded her, as real as the avocado trees, as real as the man beside her.

Ben had fallen silent, but she was content just to be with him. As they walked along, the soles of their shoes crunched over the thin layer of decomposed granite covering the soft earthen roadway; she heard no other sound.

At a curve in the road, Ben stepped off the path to check a length of irrigation pipe. He straightened, then reached up to grab a leaf off a tree.

"See how the leaves are hanging down?" He stroked the leaf tenderly with his thumb. "The trees are a little stressed. It's been another dry year and it shows."

"Can't you just irrigate more?"

He gave a short laugh. "It's not that simple." He stepped back onto the path and threw the leaf aside.

She fell into step beside him, sorry the easy mood had passed. "I know. People are selling agricultural land all the time because it's too expensive to keep it—" she couldn't think of the word she needed and stumbled "—you know, keep it growing things."

He supplied the word. "Productive."

She gave him a grateful glance. "That's right, keep it productive. And the rewards for selling out to the developers are too great."

"Selling out is the proper term for it, all right. But I'm hanging in there. All I need is one decent crop." He spoke fiercely, as if he expected her to argue about it.

She was way too savvy not to know that one decent crop was just the beginning of what he needed, but no way could she debate the subject.

They walked for a few more minutes, but the easy feeling was gone. Ahead she could see the barn and the vehicles parked beneath the trees. She didn't want to leave with this strain between them. "Ben," she began hesitantly, "I . . . I'm sorry."

"For what?"

"For . . . whatever."

They slowed before the barn. He turned glittering blue eyes toward her. "You didn't do anything. I was thinking about something else."

She felt a flash of jealousy, and then was ashamed of herself. "Want to talk about it?"

He shook his shaggy head with finality. "No. I—"

The kitten hurtled through the barn door and Juliana fell back with a gasp of surprise, crashing into Ben's chest. He caught her around the waist, holding her steady until she regained her composure.

"It's just Freeloader," she said breathlessly. She stared down at the sleek little creature twining itself around their ankles. She tilted her head to smile at Ben over her shoulder. His face was very near and she could see the deep crease in his right cheek, the faint cleft in his chin.

He glared at the kitten. "I don't know why it keeps hanging around here." He released her and started to walk away, but the kitten darted between his feet.

He stumbled and caught his balance, swearing. He drew back one foot, and for a horrified instant, she thought he was going to kick the kitten across the barnyard.

She gave a little cry of protest and started forward with outstretched arms. Before she could intervene, he scooped the kitten up in his big hands and lifted it to eye level, his expression fierce.

"Damn freeloading cat," he said explosively, then pressed his cheek against the lustrous fur. Juliana watched, not knowing what to say or do to help him.

"DID YOU EVER STOP to realize that your life is completely at the mercy of 'ifs'? *If* you'd done this—*if* you hadn't done that . . ."

Ben stopped pacing and glared at Juliana, who sat quietly on the bench against the barn wall. The kitten on her lap yawned and stretched, flexing its claws in the fabric of her jeans. With one hand she idly stroked the little creature, but her attention was on Ben.

He felt as if a gate had creaked open somewhere deep inside, releasing all the pain and guilt and torment. He couldn't stand still; he started walking again, back and forth, back and forth.

"If I hadn't taken the job in San Francisco. . . . But I was a cocky bastard. Supercop! I could do it all because I had it all—beautiful wife, fine son, bright future. Man, I felt like a king. Then I killed a man."

She caught her breath, but it barely registered with him. He'd never said these things out loud before and he couldn't stop now that he'd started. At the moment he wasn't interested in her reaction to his words, only his own.

"The guy I iced was some derelict suspected of armed robbery. He was reaching inside this old rag of a coat and

I thought he was going for a gun so I shot the son of a bitch. Turned out he had this minuscule amount of grass. I guess he thought he was busted and was going to try to eat it or throw it away or some damned thing."

He groaned. "I went on suspension while the department investigated, which means I sat around all day thinking about it. They finally cleared me but I couldn't seem to get past my own conscience. Lord, I was supposed to protect the weak, not blow them away. It shook the hell out of me.

"A month after I went back to work, a woman I was interviewing on a drug case was gunned down right in front of me. I'd just got through telling her that she could speak freely— 'Trust us,' I said. 'We'll protect you.'"

He halted in the shadow of the barn. For a moment he closed his eyes, his jaws aching with stress.

"You're too hard on yourself."

He glared at her through half-closed eyes. "I wasn't hard enough. I almost quit for good after that, but everybody made excuses for me. If I'd quit, Melanie and Jimmy would be alive today."

She flinched and for a moment stopped stroking the sleeping kitten. "Your wife and child?"

"Yes."

Her head dipped and she moistened her lips. "I'm sorry. I just assumed you were divorced."

"Yeah, well, you assumed wrong." He spoke roughly, because he still couldn't talk about it calmly. Up until now, he hadn't been able to talk about it, period. "After the accident . . . after it was too late to matter, I quit the force. I was drunk for a couple of years...a bum. Alcohol was my amnesia pill—when I couldn't stand to remember, I drank myself insensible."

Finally the words were winding down. He felt empty, as if the bad feelings had tumbled out with the words, leaving a black, empty hole. "I didn't know it was possible to get as low as I got and still be human. Then one day. . ."

"What?" she encouraged.

Through the gathering dusk her face swam before him, indistinct, but nonetheless very real. Her scarf had slipped down around her shoulders, and her cropped hair and big eyes gave her a gamin air. He felt such a flash of affinity that he strained to find some similarity between her and the woman he had loved and married. He found none.

"Then what happened?" she repeated.

He shook his head. "Nothing." He didn't want to tell her about his mother's efforts to rehabilitate him. He supposed he'd already said too much, but instead of regret, he felt almost giddy with relief.

She looked up at him, her lips slightly parted as if she held her breath, her expression tender.

He spoke carelessly, but his gravelly voice sounded even huskier than usual. "Jeez, I don't know what got me started. Want to come in and see if we can find anything to eat?"

And so they went inside the house and she prepared cheese omelets topped with sour cream and slices of soft, ripe avocado. They ate on the deck overlooking the Pacific Ocean. After a while the awkwardness created by the unexpected intimacy of Ben's revelations passed and they relaxed into a semblance of easy companionship.

When the stars began to twinkle overhead, he sent her on her way as if nothing had happened.

JULIANA WENT BACK the next day, and the day after that. She rose each morning with new purpose, convinced against all reason that with her help, the Ware avocado grove would not only survive but prosper.

Now she hummed happily to herself as she carried the big jar of sun tea into Ben's spotless kitchen. He was unloading supplies from the truck and lugging them inside the barn, and she figured he could use a cool drink right about now.

The barn hadn't been used for livestock in years, although once the Wares had kept riding horses and a milk cow or two. Mrs. Ware had sold the animals after her husband's death four years ago. Ben used the structure mainly for storage.

A tall glass in each hand, she entered the barn through the big double doors at one end. Identical doors opened at the opposite end, offering a straight shot through from either direction. Ben stood in front of the far opening, his body backlit, in the act of shaking the dust and leafy debris out of his chambray work shirt. He gave her a quick grin, which she hardly noticed as her attention zeroed in on his bare torso.

Smooth golden skin flowed over flexing and unflexing muscles in his arms and chest as he moved. Dust motes danced in the shaft of sunlight that streamed over and around him. He tossed the shirt onto a stanchion. Lifting both hands, he dipped his head to ruffle bits of leaves and twigs from his unruly blond mane.

The entire scene struck her as wildly exotic and alien, more like a misty golden watercolor than reality. The shadowed musculature of his body, the warm shine of his hair gilded by sunlight, the slight curve of his mouth...all combined in a dreamlike haze before her dazzled eyes.

She swallowed hard, wondering what in the hell was causing her to react so strangely—and so strongly. It was more than just this sudden awareness of his body. She'd seen and admired that before; he often stripped off his shirt while working in the groves.

He stepped deeper into the barn's shadowed interior, and the shaft of golden light silhouetted his long, heavily muscled legs, planted solidly apart.

Good grief, what's happening to me? She felt as if she'd been kicked in the stomach. She couldn't breathe; she couldn't speak.

But he could. "You're not going to just stand there and let the ice melt, are you?" He started toward her.

The pulse in her throat hammered so strongly that her voice almost failed her. "I'm sorry." She thrust a glass into his hand. "Here." Without another word, she turned and left the barn.

She heard his footsteps behind her. Still shaken, she dropped onto the bench in the shade of the front wall of the barn. He lowered his tall frame beside her and at last she risked another glance.

She saw Ben, only Ben. Not that godlike creature who'd stunned her, back there inside the barn. Not some stranger; *Ben*. She smiled in relief and he smiled back. Whatever she'd felt back there, he obviously hadn't. Thank goodness. And now, neither did she. Put it down to a temporary aberration.

He took a swig of tea and leaned back against the wall. He stretched out his legs, his shoes stirring up dust. "You're becoming about halfway useful around here," he said.

She made a face at him. "Thanks for nothing."

For a moment he remained silent. Then he slanted her a guarded glance. "I might even miss you when you go back to work. Which should be soon."

She stiffened and her heart began to pound. "Don't push." She stared down at the drink in her hand. The air was so dry that no moisture had condensed on the glass.

"Juli." His low gravelly voice coaxed. "You know it's time."

"I don't know any such thing." She sprang to her feet and walked quickly toward the house, intending to leave her glass in the kitchen and go home. If he didn't want her around, she wouldn't force herself on him.

A dusty-blue pickup turned into the yard and Juliana came to an awkward halt. She'd left her scarf on the front seat of her car. Automatically, she lifted one hand to her head in her usual gesture of denial.

The pickup stood between her and the house. She was, in effect, trapped. She heard Ben behind her.

"Hang in there," he said softly. "It's only a neighbor."

Juliana realized that. She'd known Opal Rudnick slightly for years, but wasn't any happier to see her because of that.

Opal crawled out of the cab of the truck and lumbered toward them. A big-boned woman with a crown of snowy hair, she moved with little grace but plenty of energy. She had to be in her late sixties, Juliana supposed, but the round face betrayed few signs of age.

"Howdy, folks." Opal halted in front of the pair, battered cowboy boots raising puffs of dust. She wore faded jeans and a plaid shirt with the sleeves rolled above the elbow.

Ben touched Juliana's elbow lightly. "Opal, do you know Juliana Robinson?"

Opal waved him silent. "Since she was Juliana Malone. Her daddy was the first person me and Cloyd met when we come out here from Missouri. He sold us our place when she was just a little bit of a thing." She grinned at Juliana. "How you doin', girl? Sorry to hear you been sick."

Juliana's lips parted in surprise, her perplexed glance flying to Ben's face. He nodded reassuringly. "Th-thank you," she managed. "I'm fine now. If you'll excuse me, I'll just put this glass in the kitchen."

She edged away from Ben and headed toward the house. When would she ever get over this feeling of panic around all but a precious few?

"Just a minute, hon."

At Opal's command, Juliana halted in confusion.

"You still in real estate?"

Juliana turned slowly. "Yes."

"Thought so. If you're anything at all like your daddy, you're purty good at it."

"Why, I...yes, I do all right." *But I'm nothing at all like my daddy.*

"Good." Opal nodded her head decisively. "I got some friends, the Burtons. You heard'a them?"

The name sounded vaguely familiar, but Juliana didn't know why. She shook her head "no."

Opal shrugged. "Don't matter. They need some real-estate advice and they need it bad. They're gettin' on in years—did I mention these are *old* friends?" She laughed at her own joke. "They're house-poor, if you know what I mean, but they've had bad experiences with you real-estate folks in the past so they're a bit leery. I told 'em I'd hunt up somebody they could trust."

Juliana smiled blankly. She rarely handled a small transaction like the sale of an individual home. She'd turned toward commercial and industrial real estate be-cause—hell, she wasn't ashamed to admit it—that's where the money was. "So . . . would you like me to recommend someone to help your friends? There are a number of good people in my office."

"Land a mercy, no!" Opal let out a cackle of laughter. "I want *you* to help 'em out your own self. I been rackin' my brains, just wishin' your daddy was still alive, and here you are. I figure it's a sign." She winked broadly. "This is Thursday—I'll send 'em in to see you at your office tomorrow afternoon, if that's all right."

Without waiting for a response, she gave Juliana a wide grin and turned back to Ben. "Now, about them Leaf Loopers—we had a real bad infestation last year so . . ."

Ben gave Juliana an eloquent shrug, his naked shoulders rising expressively as he turned to follow Opal toward the nearest row of avocado trees. He might as well have said, *You're on your own with this one.*

OPAL HELD the curly green worm on her palm and shook her head woefully. "Danged little varmints." She dropped the worm on the ground and smashed it with the toe of one boot.

She'd spent the past half hour talking avocados. Ben had listened with patient interest, as he always did—more so this time. It helped take his mind off Juliana and the extraordinary jolt he'd felt when she entered the barn a few minutes ago.

Besides, he liked Opal. The opinionated old gal also had been a close friend of his mother's. And Opal Rudnick and her husband, Cloyd, had forgotten more about avocados than Benjamin Ware would ever know, even if he held onto this land for fifty years—a possibility growing more remote every day.

Opal sighed. "It's a moot point, though. It won't be the Leaf Loopers that get you, boy."

"Then what will?" Ben arched one heavy brow, his mouth quirking up at one corner.

"Progress. It's gonna get us all." Opal shook her head in disgust.

He frowned out over the valley. "You mean developers," he said darkly.

"No, I mean progress. Civilization." She spat out the word as if it offended her, and without missing a beat, added, "You need some wasps, boy."

Ben blinked. "Wasps?"

"To get rid of them Leaf Loopers. Or you could sell 'em."

"The wasps or the Leaf Loopers?"

"Both." She laughed and pounded him on the back with a friendly fist. "And all the trees, too. Sell the whole kit 'n' caboodle before you get swallowed up by progress. Save yourself a lot of grief if you do." Suddenly she looked serious, no longer kidding around.

His gut tightened. "You trying to tell me something, Opal?"

She looked past him, out over the land. For a split second she looked her age, and more. "Just that me and Cloyd...we see the handwriting on the wall." She touched his arm with unexpectedly gentle fingers. "Come over here, boy."

She led him to the edge of the terraced level high on the rim of the valley. She threw out one arm in a sweeping gesture.

"What do you see, boy?"

He examined the peaceful scene before him. "Your place over there to the right...the Maxwell farm and Buena Suerte Canyon Road. South and west is Summerhill."

She nodded. "And do you see those little patches of concrete down there, littering up the landscape? Building pads, boy. Houses, people...how much longer you think we can keep swimmin' against the tide?"

Ben's jaw tightened to the point of pain. "I just got here. I'm not ready to let go."

Her shoulders slumped. "Me, neither. And I been here a hundred years, seems like. But this will be our last season. Right after the pickin's finished this summer, Cloyd and me are givin' up the ghost."

Her laugh had a hollow ring to it. "And we don't care who we sell to—that Godfrey fellow or whoever. We just want enough money to take care of us in our old age."

She brightened, and nudged him in the ribs with one elbow. "Old age is just down the road. Another twenty, thirty years, way I reckon'. Me and Cloyd, we're gonna have us some fun in the meantime! To hell with Leaf Loopers, say I!"

WHERE IS HE? Juliana paced around the kitchen, unable to settle down. He had to get her out of this. No way was she going to get involved with some old goofy couple with house problems. It would be a project long on time and short on profit.

Being compared with her father didn't improve her humor, either. When that happened, she always came out on the short end of the stick. Hardly fair, when she'd made ten times more money ten times faster. But all anybody ever remembered about her father was what a nice guy he was, not that he was frequently late with his own mortgage payments.

Wait a minute. I said I wouldn't measure everything in dollars and cents anymore. I said I was going to change.

Change, yes, but there's no need to get ridiculous about it, she told herself, peeking through the curtain for the umpteenth time. Ben and Opal had at last returned from the grove and now stood talking beneath the big shade trees.

Juliana slapped the curtains down and whirled away from the window. She had to find something to occupy herself or go mad.

The answer stared her in the face. *This is a kitchen—I'll bake something*, she decided. She'd learned to bake from her mother, a cook of some local renown. Juliana had grown up expecting to follow in her mother's footsteps—wonderful wife, wonderful mother, wonderful cook and housekeeper.

Wonderful at juggling bills and putting off creditors.

Water under the bridge, she reminded herself as she opened a cabinet door and surveyed the shelves.

Canisters of flour and sugar lined up next to a lazy susan loaded with flavored extracts, food colors, and a bottle of those wretched little silver decorating candies that looked and tasted like ball bearings. Paige had loved them as a child, poking them onto every cookie that came within her reach.

Had Mrs. Ware bought the silver decorations to please her grandson? *Don't think about that*, Juliana ordered herself. She resumed her inventory: vegetable shortening on the top shelf, eggs and milk in the refrigerator. She pulled the cartons out and set them on the counter.

Rosalie Malone had baked a wonderful loaf of avocado bread. The decision made, Juliana pulled down a mixing bowl and measuring cups, then rummaged around in a drawer until she located measuring spoons. She felt better already, although she handled the utensils gingerly to protect her fingernails.

Paige had shaped her mother's nails and applied a coat of clear polish. Juliana stood in awe of her nails. Eventually one of them was going to break and then she'd have to cut the other nine, but in the meantime she took a quite shameless pride in them.

Okay, flour, sugar, egg . . . or was that eggs?

She frowned, uncomfortably aware of a tightening in her chest. How much sugar? How many eggs?

She'd used this recipe since childhood. She could recite it in her sleep: egg (or eggs), mashed avocado, buttermilk, vegetable oil, flour, sugar, baking soda, baking powder, salt and chopped nuts—and she didn't have the first clue how much of anything.

She felt the clammy touch of cold sweat on her forehead. *Be calm*, she cautioned herself. *You're pressing too hard. It will come if you just relax.*

Like everything else? She couldn't remember what the mortgage rate was when she went into the hospital, for the love of heaven. She couldn't remember dates. She'd pay bills and forget the date between writing the first check and the second.

She'd go by looks, she decided. She wouldn't let this . . . this temporary aberration get the best of her. She picked up the sugar canister and poured a stream of sparkling crystals into the mixing bowl, hesitated, considered, then dumped in a bit more.

Eggs. Two sounded about right. What the hell was the difference, one egg or two? It wouldn't ruin anything. And salt came in pinches; that was easy enough.

She hadn't found any vegetable oil so she decided to melt some of the solid shortening. Warily she eyed the heavy can on the very edge of the top shelf. If she stretched . . .

Rising on tiptoes, she extended her arm, finally managing to graze the side of the heavy can with her fingertips. She stretched to the maximum, coaxing the can toward her by rotating it gently. There! The bottom of the can began to appear over the edge of the shelf. If she could just work it out far enough to get her thumb beneath it she could balance the can on one hand and—

The kitchen door opened behind her, startling her and shattering her concentration. With a frightened cry, she jerked her arm down. The heavy shortening can wavered, then toppled off the shelf and hurtled down at her.

6

BEN LEAPED FORWARD, his shout of warning lost in her scream. For one sickening second he thought the can would surely strike her on the head. But she threw up her arms and the can careened off one elbow to splat against the kitchen linoleum, a hair's breadth from her right foot.

She buried her face in her hands and stood there, her whole body trembling. He reached her in two long strides, his heart banging painfully inside his chest. Grabbing her by the wrists, he pulled her arms down so he could see her face. "Thank God you're all right!" he exclaimed.

Only now that he could see her expression, he was no longer sure she *was* all right. She didn't appear to hear him or see him; he read total denial in her blank expression.

He released her wrists and her arms dropped to her sides. Catching her by the shoulders, he gave her a light, impatient shake.

"Snap out of it, Juliana," he commanded. "It's okay—you're not hurt." Relief made his voice gruff.

Sudden comprehension flooded her face, and her lips parted. *She's going to start screaming*, he realized. *She's about to lose it.*

So he kissed her.

He didn't think about possible consequences; he simply acted. Her lips felt cool beneath his, and very, very soft. Very, very defenseless... And then she yanked back, her eyes wide and frightened.

"It's all right," he whispered, holding her lightly by the shoulders. "I don't know any other way to comfort you."

"Oh." She caught her breath on the word, then sighed and swayed toward him.

He pulled her into his arms and looked down into her face as her eyelids drifted closed. So he kissed her again.

This time her mouth felt warm and alive, but with an appealing uncertainty. He hadn't planned on letting passion creep in, but he found himself coaxing her lips apart. She hesitated and then yielded to him. His tongue plunged inside; desire ripped through him with the sudden full joining of their mouths.

He gathered her pliant form closer as heat curled his stomach into an aching knot. He moved his hips against hers in time to the urgent stroking of his tongue.

Comfort was suddenly the farthest thing from his mind. And from hers.

Juliana slipped her arms around his neck, dizzy and disoriented, but pleasantly so. All the powerful anxiety of the last few minutes seemed to disintegrate beneath the potency of his kiss. Cold chills ran up and down her spine, her arms. Her trembling knees threatened to collapse entirely.

This can't be happening, she thought, her mind teeming with a million implications. Taken completely by surprise, she'd had no time to prepare her usual defenses. For a woman accustomed to being in control of situations and her own emotions, being in control of neither was a terrifying—and heady—experience.

The kiss deepened—his doing or hers? He dropped his hand from the small of her back to her buttocks, drawing her even more tightly against him, and she felt the strength of his arousal. She rose onto tiptoes, trying to lose herself in him, her thighs pressing against his, her hips responding to the rhythmic thrust of his.

He dragged his lips away and lifted his head. His breath labored in his throat, but then, so did hers. They simply stood there in each other's arms, as if neither could figure a graceful way to move either forward or back.

After a moment she cleared her throat and her gaze fell from his face to the strong column of his throat. She could see the throb of his pulse beneath the smooth bronzed skin. She swallowed hard. "I'm sorry I . . . overreacted. If that can had hit me, it could have killed me."

"It could have killed Arnold what's-his-name, if it'd hit him on the head. It was a dangerous thing to do, knocking it off the shelf."

He sounded exactly the same as he always did, a detail wildly at odds with the fact that they still stood locked in an intimate embrace.

"Yes, but . . ." She shuddered. Better to concentrate on physical danger than the emotional peril in which she found herself. "I live in terror of accidents. I go around ducking and dodging and covering my head with my arms."

"That'll pass. Just give it time. When your hair grows a little longer, things'll get back to normal."

"But when will that be?" She bit her lower lip. "Sometimes I wonder if things will ever be normal again. Will I ever feel comfortable around people? Will I ever work up the nerve to go back to the office?"

"Tomorrow. You promised."

"I *didn't* promise. Opal *assumed*."

He knew that stubborn expression by now and recognized a fight in the making. Maybe a good fight was what she needed to take her mind off what had truly been a terrifying near disaster.

He tightened his grip on her waist. She leaned away from him, her back curving, which brought her hips more firmly into contact with his. *Keep it up*, he thought grimly, *feels great*. Damn, it'd been a hell of a long time since he'd got worked up by a woman, and he was definitely worked up—and getting more so.

Pay attention here, Ware. He cleared his throat. "Opal assumed you were your father's daughter. I don't think she was wrong."

Her outrage pleased him; she fairly sputtered, and bright color washed into her pale face.

"You don't know anything about it." She braced her hands on his arms and shoved. "Will you . . . just . . . *turn me loose?*"

"All you had to do was ask."

He released her so suddenly that she stumbled into the table, reaching back to steady herself with her hands. She started to speak, but instead gasped as if in pain.

Instantly contrite, he stepped toward her. "What is it? Are you all right?"

She looked on the verge of tears. "Now look what you've done!" She held out one trembling hand.

He stared down at it in consternation. On the end of her arm he saw a perfectly natural hand. It had five fingers just like most hands. He looked more closely, frowning.

It also had five very long nails, one of which now dangled by the fingernail equivalent of a thread.

JULIANA SAT at Ben's kitchen table, snipping her fingernails with a metal clipper and seething. But beneath her very genuine anger and disappointment over the untimely demise of her fantastic fingernails, there lurked a vague feeling of relief.

Relief that something had distracted her from a sudden, burning, overwhelming awareness of Ben's tremendous physical appeal. Even now, ruthlessly divesting herself of this last and only vanity, she still tingled with new sensations.

He sat across from her, drinking a can of soda, his expression stoic. He acted exactly the same, but to her he looked completely different: eyes bluer, shoulders wider, dimples deeper, and—heaven help her—everything sexier.

A whole lot sexier.

Don't look—clip, she ordered herself.

When she was short-nailed again, she glared down at the clippings on the paper napkin before her. "Shi-oooot," she said.

"Heard you the first time." He clapped down the can and stood up. "Let's go to the mall."

"Forget it." She hadn't been to the mall since her release from the hospital and she sure as hell had no reason to go now.

His heavy brows, darker than his sun-streaked blond hair, lowered threateningly. "Don't be a pain in the butt, Juliana."

She ran the pads of her thumbs over the still-sharp edges of her newly devastated nails. As a delaying tactic, it failed miserably; he simply took her arm, lifted her out of the chair and stood her on her feet.

The matter seemed somehow settled.

HE DRAGGED HER behind him through the department store, her hand engulfed in his big paw.

"But I don't *want* a wig," she insisted, trying to dig in her heels.

"Yes, you do. You're just too damned stubborn to admit it."

He stopped at the edge of the wig and hat department, clamping one arm around her to keep her at his side.

"Damn it, Ben! You're a big bully."

"Yeah, yeah, I know." He sounded unimpressed. He pointed to a series of glass shelves displaying wigs of many colors and styles. "Do you like any of those?"

Before she could respond, a carefully groomed saleswoman approached. "I'll be right with you," she said pleasantly. She continued on to a woman who sat at the small vanity table provided for customers trying on wigs.

"I'm getting out of here," Juliana whispered.

Ben shushed her. She gave him a dirty look while he openly eavesdropped on the saleswoman and her customer.

"I—I'd like to try on a wig," the seated woman said. She was about Juliana's age, perhaps a few years younger, and she, too, wore a scarf over her head and wrapped around her throat. She smiled apologetically. "I recently started chemotherapy treatments and they've sort of . . . my hair . . ."

Hesitantly she untied the scarf and loosened it, without removing it entirely. "My natural color is dishwater blond." She laughed nervously. "I kind of like the wig over there—the fluffy one. Do you have that in a light brown?"

"I certainly do. It's one of our newest styles."

The clerk helped the woman slip the wig on. She'd lost tufts of hair all over her head; it was awful, ever so much worse than simply having your head shaved, Juliana admitted to herself.

With the wig firmly in place, the woman smiled broadly into the mirror, then glanced up at the saleswoman for confirmation.

"Perfect," the saleswoman pronounced with a smile.

"I like it, too. But I'm afraid my husband may think this color's a little too light." The woman frowned into the mirror, chewing on her bottom lip. "He wanted to come with me, but this was something I had to do for myself."

Juliana turned so abruptly that she plowed into Ben's firm chest. *She* hadn't wanted to do it for herself; Ben had had to drag her in here kicking and screaming. "I'm a bitch," she muttered, her voice shaky.

"That's true." He dipped one eyelid in a conspiratorial wink.

He released his hold on her—she could leave now, if she chose, but she knew she wouldn't. If that poor woman had the nerve to face up to it, Juliana Robinson sure as hell did.

With assistance from the saleswoman, the choice was made and a smiling customer walked away a few minutes later, her hair picture perfect. A paisley scarf trailed from the pocket of her jacket.

Somehow she seemed different, more self-assured than the woman who'd furtively removed her scarf to bare her humiliation a few moments ago. And humiliation it was; Juliana understood that only too well. Although in this enlightened age a woman's hair might no longer be considered her crowning glory, still it remained a powerful symbol of femininity.

The saleswoman gave a satisfied sigh and turned toward Juliana. "Sorry to keep you waiting. How may I help you?"

Juliana took a deep breath. "I'd like a wig," she said firmly. "I—" She glanced at Ben, suddenly thinking how foolish she felt comparing her situation to the one they'd just encountered. She would recover. It was just a matter of time. But chemotherapy could go on and on, with no guarantee of success.

So she said, "I had a haircut recently that didn't work out and I need something to hide it while it grows back."

Then she found herself sitting before the mirror, examining an auburn wig that fell smoothly into a short twenties' bob with full bangs and fitted nape. She yanked off her dark glasses and scarf and with clumsy eagerness, positioned the wig over her own super-short hair. Her questioning eyes met those of the saleswoman in the mirror.

The woman's face was slack with surprise. "Boy, that was some haircut. You should sue!"

Juliana laughed. "I was kidding about that." She adjusted the wig and smoothed a wing of hair over one cheek. "I had brain surgery."

"Oh, I'm so sorry."

"It was nothing." Juliana's gaze met Ben's in the mirror and she smiled. She felt suddenly and unexpectedly wonderful. Funny what a new hairdo—or new hair—could do for a woman.

She wore the wig. As she and Ben headed for the exit, a display mannequin wearing the perfect dress to go with her new "look" caught her attention. The dress, gauzy and gray, was sleeveless with a dropped waist and jagged handkerchief hem—a costume straight out of a silent movie, she thought as she paused to admire it.

"It's gorgeous," she sighed, lifting the skirt and letting it fall back in a graceful flutter. Unfortunately, it didn't fit her image. "Let's go," she said briskly, turning toward the door.

"Wha 'da'ya mean, let's go?" Ben caught her arm and drew her up short. "Try it on."

"Are you kidding?" What she meant was, "Are you nuts?"

He looked pained. "You like it. I like it. Go put it on."

"It's not my style," she argued. "I've never worn anything like that in my life. I'm more the tailored type."

"Bull. Save us an argument and just put the damned thing on."

She couldn't resist his logic. Once she donned the dress, she couldn't resist *it*, either. So she bought it, feeling downright daring as she wrote the check.

And happy. Happy enough to burst. Once out on the sidewalk, she whirled around in front of Ben and stopped him with one of her hands flat against his chest.

"Thank you." Her palm tingled, where it pressed against his chambray shirt. She withdrew her hand quickly. "I wouldn't even have tried that dress on without your unsolicited advice."

"That's probably true." His face wore a wary expression, as if he expected her to add a "but" there on the end.

The silence—the tension—stretched taut between them. She broke first, turning to lead the way through the early evening dusk toward her car. She licked dry lips, feeling breathless and shaky. Without comment, he fell into step beside her.

She gave him a tentative smile over one shoulder. "This has been a great day, in spite of everything." She felt the need to talk, to connect with him on some level, however superficial.

He pulled her car keys from his pocket and unlocked the passenger door of the Mercedes. "Didn't start out too well, as I remember. First Opal shook you up, then you almost caught five pounds of shortening with your head."

A chill snaked down her back at the memory, but she shook it off and climbed into the car. "Yes, but after that it got good," she said with determined cheer.

He slid behind the wheel and shifted on the seat to look at her. She met his gaze, feeling like a young girl, happy and excited and no longer trying to control the situation or hide her feelings.

He reached out and drew the fingers of one hand lightly over her cheek. "I think I'd better get you home," he said gruffly. "Tomorrow's a big day."

"Tomorrow?" She was so enthralled by his fleeting touch that for a moment the significance of his words didn't sink in. Then they did.

"Oh, that," she said unhappily. She didn't want to think about tomorrow and Opal's friends, partly because she couldn't bear for today to end. But maybe it didn't need to, at least not yet. "Ben, do you have any plans for this evening?" she asked impulsively.

He started the car. "No." He gave her a narrow look over his shoulder. "Why?"

She hesitated. She wanted to spend the evening with him, it was as simple as that, only. . . *Get a grip, Juliana. You're about to do something stupid.*

Because everything about him drew her now—the way he looked, the way his gravelly voice sent shivers up and down her spine, the way his harsh expression softened when he laughed. . . .

Why had it taken her so long to acknowledge his special qualities? For a heady moment she stared at his strong profile, admiring the straight nose and wicked curve of his mouth.

I'll bet he's spectacular in bed.

She gulped and looked quickly away. Never in her life had she entertained such blatant speculations about any man. In fact, the entire topic of sex occupied very little of her time or attention. She'd always believed sex was something she could live without.

Lord knows, she had. She did. She was.

"Hey, wake up."

She reined in her rampaging thoughts. "I'm sorry. I was just thinking." She swallowed hard. "Why don't we pick up Paige and all go out to dinner? It'll give me a chance to try out my new look in public. My treat." With Paige along, they'd soon be back on the old, comfortable footing.

Did he hesitate just a shade too long? "I suppose it'd be okay. It's been a while since I saw the kid. But I'll buy."

"No, it's my idea so it's my treat." Relieved, Juliana settled back in her seat.

They argued good-naturedly about it the rest of the way.

THEY ATE CHINESE, Ben ordering for all of them. They shared the various dishes family style—moo shi pork, the thin Chinese version of tortillas filled with meat and vegetables and rolled up like a burrito, followed by shrimp with cashew nuts, tomato beef chow mein, and in deference to Paige, sweet and sour pork.

They ate, they drank hot tea, and they talked. Like old and dear friends, Juliana thought as she leaned back in her chair, relaxed and happy.

The waiter arrived with a plate of fortune cookies, and Juliana poured more tea.

"I'm too full for a fortune cookie," she announced. "That was really wonderful, Ben. How did you learn so much about Oriental food?"

"A natural talent," he said with ostentatious modesty, breaking open a cookie.

"Ha!" Paige gave him a mock-scornful look. "He learned from his wife." She grinned at Juliana. "She lived in the City before they got married—that's what people in San Francisco call it, 'the City.' She knew all the best restaurants in Chinatown, all those weird places with the stiff brown ducks hanging by their necks in the windows."

Ben looked startled, as if thrown off by the girl's teasing remarks. Juliana felt a quick stab of jealousy, and ruthlessly beat it back. But she couldn't help feeling resentful that Ben had confided such personal details of his former life, not to her but to Paige.

Or had he? *Have I just forgotten?* Juliana wondered, suddenly confused and unsure.

Ben gave Paige a stern look. "I can see I'm going to have to watch what I say in front of you," he groused. "Everything can and will be used against me."

Paige made a face at him, then gave her mother a conspiratorial glance. "That's cop talk," she said lightly. With barely concealed impatience, she watched Ben pull the fortune out of his cookie. "Well, what's it say?"

"It says, 'Beware of beautiful woman with ulterior motive and silver tongue.'"

Their easy relationship was starting to grate on Juliana, even though she understood its source. They had gone through something together that she had caused but not shared—and she resented the hell out of it.

Paige leaned forward and snatched the slip of paper from his fingers. She glanced at it, then gave him a triumphant grin. "That's not what it says! It says, 'The next full moon will beam happiness your way.'"

Juliana shook her head and forced herself to rejoin the party. "What a faker."

Ben shrugged and popped a crispy bit of cookie into his mouth. "So sue me."

Paige relaxed back in her chair and darted her mother a quickly assessing glance. "You look like you're in a good mood, Mama," she observed too casually.

Juliana arched one brow. "That's a fairly safe assumption."

She waited for Paige to go on. Instead, the girl picked up a fortune cookie and turned it over and over in her hands.

Something was definitely on Paige's mind, had been all evening, Juliana realized. She waited patiently for whatever little problem her daughter might bring up.

"So," Ben said finally, breaking the silence. He, too, seemed to sense the sudden tension. "How's school, Paige?"

She looked grateful. "Fine. No problems, Ben."

"And your volunteer work at the hospital?"

Her face became animated and excitement brightened her eyes. "I really love it," she declared. "There's so much to learn. And everyone's so nice—the staff and the patients, too."

Juliana smiled at her daughter, wondering how long it was going to take her to get over this newest enthusiasm. "Just don't let your school work suffer," she advised tolerantly.

Paige glanced quickly at Ben, who was busy trying to extract fortunes from the remaining cookies without breaking them. "Actually," she said, giving her mother a cautious glance, "that's something I've been meaning to talk to you about."

Ben looked up sharply; Paige recoiled, her wide eyes focused on him. "I know I said I'd wait, Ben, but—"

Juliana's pulse raced, spreading anxiety throughout her body. "What's going on here?" she demanded more sharply than she intended.

Paige gulped hard. "You are in a good mood, right?"

"I was!" Juliana got a grip on herself. It was ridiculous to react before there was anything to react to. "No, I *am* in a good mood."

"And I know you've mellowed since you got out of the hospital. You're not nearly so uptight."

Uptight? Not a descriptive phrase Juliana enjoyed hearing applied to herself, even in the past tense. "Let's stop talking about me and start talking about you," she suggested.

"Sure, what am I worried about?" Paige gave a hollow laugh. "Mama, I've decided what I want to do with my life."

"Just what is that supposed to mean?" But Juliana had a sneaking suspicion she knew. She braced herself.

"I want to be a nurse. I want to help people, Mama. I want to save lives." Paige drew in an enormous breath and slumped down in her chair, her expression a study in relief.

Juliana's response was automatic and uncensored. *"Have you lost your mind?"*

Paige recoiled. "I thought there was at least a chance you'd understand."

"What's to understand?" Juliana threw up her hands in helpless disbelief. "You want to throw away your potential to empty bedpans?"

"My potential?" Paige half rose from her chair. "If I have any potential, I can't think of a better use for it than helping other people."

"Paige, Paige." Juliana shook her head in despair. She forced herself to speak calmly. "Honey, I know you're grateful to the medical profession and so am I, but that doesn't mean you have to go off the deep end about it. There are other ways to say thanks. You don't have to throw away all your plans for a career in business."

"Not my plans, *your* plans."

Now it was Juliana's turn to recoil. "That's not true!"

Paige thrust out her lower lip. "It is true. I was only majoring in business to please you. Now I know what I really want to do and you can't stop me. It's my life, Mama!"

It's my life, Mama! How many mothers had flinched at hearing those words, Juliana wondered, including her own.

Giddy with anxiety, Juliana clutched her hands together in her lap. That her beautiful and intelligent child would even consider throwing everything away to give shots and enemas was inconceivable.

Ben had stayed out of it to this point, but now he let out his breath in a disgusted snort. "This isn't getting us anywhere," he said flatly. "Why don't you both calm down?"

"I'm perfectly calm," Juliana said in a tone dripping icicles.

"Well, I'm not!" Paige swung her outraged glance between her mother and Ben. "I told you she'd be like this!"

He shook his head. "And I told you not to spring it on her until the time was right. What did you expect?"

"Hold it!" Juliana couldn't believe what she was hearing. "You two have discussed this behind my back? I could almost understand if you'd talked to your father, but Ben's not even part of the family."

Paige lifted her chin. "He is as far as I'm concerned." She turned her face toward him, quick tears sparkling in her eyes. "I owe him more than you can possibly know, Mother. He was there when I needed him. He put his arms around me when I cried and he helped me keep going when I didn't think I could."

"Paige—" Juliana's voice cracked.

"No! It's time you heard this." Paige's young face convulsed. "If it hadn't been for him, I'd have lost this entire semester at school—I'd have lost my mind! So his opinion means a lot to me, and he doesn't see anything wrong with nurses. Neither does Daddy."

Juliana groaned. "I guess everybody knew but good old Mom."

"Well, Daddy's certainly more reasonable than you are. He thinks medicine is a . . . a noble calling!"

Looking at the girl's outraged face, Juliana's own anger began to fade. She felt hopelessly outnumbered, not to mention misunderstood. "Medicine *is* a noble calling," she agreed. "I never meant to imply otherwise. Nursing just isn't the thing I want for my child. Long hours, low pay, low prestige—"

"And a chance to help people when they need it most—that's what's important to me. But if it'll make you feel any better, I've been looking into it and nursing offers better pay and more opportunity than ever before. Why can't you be proud of me? You shouldn't be trying to talk me out of it."

Paige turned vulnerable hazel eyes on her mother. Juliana tried to withstand the appeal she saw there but her resolve weakened.

Ben shifted, looking uncomfortable, and cleared his throat. "The two of you don't have to decide the course of Paige's life right here and now," he said, his tone coaxing. "Why not sleep on it and—"

"Will you let me handle this?" Juliana, nerves frazzled, spoke bluntly. She couldn't believe that while she was flat on her back in a hospital bed, he'd usurped her place in her daughter's heart, and so she turned on him now. "You had no right to go behind my back and influence my child."

"Mother, he didn't!"

Ben's sarcastic smile deepened the creases in his lean cheeks. "She knows I didn't, Paige. She's just pissed and taking it out on me." He leaned back in his chair, hooking his thumbs on the pockets of his Levi's. His expression remained stoic. "Hit me again," he invited Juliana. "I can take it."

Seething, Juliana considered her options quickly. Nursing was completely unacceptable for Paige, but if the girl was interested in medicine— *why of course!* Juliana felt so relieved she almost laughed aloud. "Paige, if you want a career in medicine . . . why not become a doctor?"

Paige uttered a furious squeal and jumped to her feet. Juliana rose with her. They faced each other across the table. Ben looked disgusted by this turn of events.

"You've just insulted nurses everywhere!" Paige declared in ringing tones.

"I've done no such thing. Doctors do even more good than nurses and they make a hell of a lot more money and have a hell of a lot more prestige."

"I'm not doing this for money or prestige!"

"That's because you've never done without them and you don't realize how important they are!"

"That does it," Ben cut in, his voice fierce. "That's exactly the kind of thing you used to say. So much for change."

"I have changed!" Her eyes felt like two burning holes in her face and she knew her lips trembled. She glanced from Paige to Ben and back again, desperate for understanding. "Look, I read the newspapers. Nurses are overworked and underpaid—everybody knows that. I don't want that kind of life for Paige."

The young face grew hard with determination. "Mother, you're a snob."

"*I am not!* But I hope I haven't lost my common sense."

"Ben!" Paige turned an anguished face toward him. "You make her understand!"

"Hey, don't look at me. Your mother's made it crystal clear that this is strictly a family quarrel." He held up his hands and shook his head, as if determined not to be drawn in again. "Include me out."

Juliana's lips thinned. "A little late for that, don't you think? Admit it—you agree with her."

"Not entirely. You see, *I* wouldn't call you a snob, Juliana." His eyes narrowed as he looked at her. "What I'd call you is a *mercenary* snob."

"And I'd call you—"

"What? Go ahead. Say it."

She couldn't meet his challenge. She sat down abruptly on her chair and drew a deep breath. "I'm too upset. I've already said things I'll regret." She looked up at her daughter. "Please sit down so we can talk about this."

"No chance." Paige snatched her purse from the table. Tears glistened on her lashes. "There's nothing to say. I'm sorry you don't approve, but it's my life and I'll do as I please."

She slammed her empty chair back into place at the table. "I'm spending the night at Daddy's. I'll be home when I calm down." She took a step, then added, "*If* I calm down."

"Don't you dare walk out on me . . . Paige!"

Paige did just that, without a backward glance. Juliana's shoulders slumped.

For several moments Ben watched her, consciously trying to keep his anger at a level high enough to block everything else.

For of all the things he'd felt for her during the course of this day, anger was by far the safest.

7

BEN SAT in the middle of the Chop-Chop Chinese restaurant and concentrated on his anger, trying to ignore everything else. In the course of this interminable day, he'd begun to experience feelings toward Juliana he'd just as soon not deal with—feelings that left him uncomfortably aware that he was, after all, mere flesh and blood.

She'd also managed to make him uncomfortably aware of how long it had been since he'd really wanted a woman. But not this woman, he kept reminding himself. She hadn't changed, not really. She was the same arrogant, selfish, social-climbing, materialistic—

A movement at his elbow distracted him and he looked around sharply. An elderly couple stood there, the woman beaming. "Juliana, is that you?" she inquired, leaning forward. "I almost didn't recognize you with your hair cut. It's adorable."

Juliana looked confused. "Oh, hello," she said in a cautious voice, the expression on her pale face guarded. Nervously she smoothed auburn strands of the wig over one cheek.

"You're looking lovely, my dear. Lost a little weight, I see—be careful not to overdo."

The man smiled. "Nice to see you, Juliana. Business good, I hope?"

"Wh-why, fine, I guess. I mean, I haven't . . ." Juliana looked at Ben, the light of wildness in her eyes.

She had no idea who these people were. Angry at her though he was, he felt a flash of sympathy. He rose and offered his hand to the man. "Ben Ware," he said. "I don't believe we've met."

The man extended his hand. "George Singleton. This is my wife, Edith. Juliana helped us sell our business a couple of years ago." He and Ben shook hands.

Comprehension transformed Juliana's face and she beamed at the couple. "George! Edith, it's so good to see you. How're the grandkids?"

Edith smiled happily. "Doing very well. But don't let us interrupt your dinner." Her knowing glance took in both Juliana and Ben. "Nice to meet you, Ben. You two have fun."

She thinks there's something going on between us, but she's wrong, Ben thought darkly as he watched the couple leave. *I'd sooner bed a cobra than—who mentioned bed?* He swung his attention back to Juliana, eager to retreat to the relative safety of acrimony.

She met his gaze without flinching, but he saw confusion in her fine hazel eyes. "Thanks. My mind went blank there for a minute. I didn't have a clue who they were."

"Think nothing of it." He tried to keep his tone chilly.

"They don't know I was sick, do they?"

"Didn't seem to."

"When something so catastrophic happens you forget the whole world isn't hanging on the outcome." She closed her eyes and shivered.

He didn't want to feel this sympathy toward her so he spoke harshly. "Feeling sorry for yourself?"

Her eyes flew wide. "No! I just . . . it was simply an observation."

"Look at the bright side. At least they didn't realize you're wearing a wig."

She recoiled and her eyes flashed. "You really are an insensitive bastard," she grated. "I'm leaving."

"Not until one of us pays the bill."

Their glances met and held.

She looked away first. "I always pay my bills," she said in a deadly calm voice.

"So do I."

They both reached for the check, but he was quicker. For a moment he thought she'd try to snatch it from his hands, but instead she retrieved the final fortune cookie on the tray. She crushed the cookie into bits, tugging out the fortune as if yanking a tooth.

She read the words out loud: "You will find true love where you least expect it." She crumpled the slip of paper into a wrinkled ball and tossed it into the ashtray. "Well, whoopty-do," she said. "I'll hold my breath."

He paid the bill, ignoring her silent disapproval. They barely spoke as she drove the Mercedes back to the ranch. Ben stared out the window at the full moon, wondering what the hell he was going to do now.

He'd already done too much. He shouldn't have kissed her, even in the name of comfort. He shouldn't have done it—if for no other reason than that he'd wanted to so badly. She'd gotten to him. Somewhere along the line, the obligation he felt toward her had turned into a hunger that clenched his gut and sharpened his tongue.

He quivered on the brink of an explosion. Muscles and fibers tightened and he shifted miserably on the plush seat. Physical discomfort translated into emotional displeasure and he glared out at the passing countryside.

"You're being damned unfair to her," he said abruptly.

She took her time answering. When she did, her words reminded him of ice cubes tinkling in a glass. "Well, now, it's not really any of your concern, is it?" She turned the car onto Buena Suerte Canyon Road.

Ben's scalp tightened with tension. "You made it my business when you keeled over in my kitchen." He could no longer control the anger vibrating in his voice. "You made it my business when you started trotting out here day after day, hanging around and getting in the way."

He heard her sharp intake of breath and was glad he'd hurt her, even with a low blow. Once started, he couldn't seem to stop. "You made it my business when you announced you'd reformed—remember that? Fortunately I didn't bet the farm on it, so I wasn't caught completely off guard when you came down heavy on Paige like that."

She braked the car beside his pickup and twisted on the seat. "I did no such thing. I simply—"

"Shut up. It's my turn." He grabbed her by the shoulders, his hands rough, but he didn't shake her as he longed to do. Instead he pressed his fingers into her flesh and half dragged her out of her leather seat.

She batted at his hands with her own. "I won't shut up! Who do you think you are anyway, bossing me around, interfering in my relationship with my daughter—"

She was angry. Good. That's the way he wanted to leave her. He shoved her aside, threw open the car door and stepped out. He leaned over to peer into the dark interior. "Go home, Juliana, and don't come back. There's nothing for you here—" he hesitated, searching for the right qualifier "—nothing that you want. You can't get your way with me on the strength of your bank account or your social standing or your daughter's profession. And I'm not going to sell my land, to you or for you."

He turned and walked away, holding his aching body carefully. He hoped he'd made her mad enough that she'd start the engine and drive away and never come back. He was in too deep. He had let her get too close.

Still, a small, vindictive corner of his soul hoped her night would be as miserable as his promised to be.

JULIANA LEAPED out of the car and ran after him. She couldn't leave it like this. If she did, he would be forever lost to her—as a friend, she reminded herself. That's all she wanted. He apparently didn't even want that.

She caught him just as he reached the kitchen door. In the light streaming from windows on either side, she grabbed his arm. It was like snagging a block of granite. The force of her own momentum swung her around into his path.

"Why are you doing this?" she cried. "I don't understand—everything was going along so well until Paige—"

"Don't blame Paige."

He spoke so wrathfully that she gasped. She wanted to cower before his righteous indignation, but forced herself to stand erect. "I'm not. I'm just trying to find out why all of a sudden you're acting as if—" her breath caught in her throat "—as if you hate me."

He took a step toward her. Startled, she took a corresponding step back. "I don't hate you," he said in a strangled voice. "Go home."

"Y-you're scaring me."

"Then get out of here!"

She wanted to; she didn't want to. His anger terrified her, but the thought of losing him was worse. His arm burned her fingers; nevertheless, she hung on doggedly. "I can't. You mean too much to me." It just slipped out and she stared at him, terrified by what she'd admitted. It came home to her with numbing force that she wasn't in control now, not even of her own words.

He took another step toward her and her heel struck the low step before the door. Automatically she stepped up. But there was no escaping his cutting words. "What the hell's that supposed to mean?"

"J-just what you think it means." *Put your arms around me—comfort me*, her thoughts compelled him. *I need what you can give me.* "Ben, your friendship..." She swallowed hard. "Your support and approval mean... a lot to me. So we disagree about Paige—can't we talk it over?"

"She's your daughter, as you keep reminding me."

"That was unfair of me. I was angry." She began to rub her hand lightly over the corded muscles of his forearm, desperately trying to reach him. She felt surrounded and overwhelmed by him, cowed by his anger and by her own need.

"That makes it all right, then," he said sarcastically. Stepping toward her, he deliberately slammed his hips against hers, pleased when she caught her breath and went rigid.

He lifted his hands to slide his fingers slowly through the strands of her wig and she stood perfectly still while he lifted it off. He tossed the wig aside and cupped the back of her head with one hand, holding her still for the hard, hot kiss he pressed upon her lips.

She melted toward him and he immediately pulled back, not yet able to get past his anger. He wanted to shock her— his hand touched her breast and she gasped. She dropped her own arms to her sides, helplessly. His eyes locked with hers as he kneaded her breast, his cupped palm barely grazing the tingling crest.

He leaned down to nuzzle the satin skin of her throat. Each new liberty increased his hunger for the next. He could feel her breast swelling to fill his hand, and the stiffness of her nipple against his palm. "You should have left when you had the chance," he grated. "Now it's too late."

"I—I don't know what you're talking about." It was a denial without conviction. She let her head fall back to rest on the kitchen door, her eyes half closing.

"Liar." His hand left her breast to tug at the top button of her pale green silk blouse. His knuckles brushed the sweet swell of her breast. She caught her breath and her eyes opened wide.

"But we're friends," she whispered, her voice breaking. She made no move to stop him. "That's all we've ever been."

"I think our relationship has just entered a new stage."

He gripped the fragile silk in one big fist and yanked. He hadn't realized until then how angry he really was; the buttons popped and he bent quickly to nuzzle the wisps of fabric aside with his searching mouth.

She sighed and pressed closer to him. Her thighs parted ever so slightly. Completely in tune with her, he thrust his knee boldly between her legs.

"Ben . . . you . . . I—"

He heard her confusion and it added to his own. No way did he want this to happen, no way did he want to face the emotional chaos that churned his gut. Angry and aroused to the point of pain, he struggled to find the strength to resist temptation—struggled and lost. He reached around behind her back and unsnapped her bra.

He slid his hands down her rib cage and around until he could balance the weight of her breasts on his hands. His thigh pressed against the juncture of her legs in a light, rubbing motion. She caught her breath and met his

triumphant gaze, her own more astonished than anything else.

He didn't blame her, not really. He couldn't believe this
was happening any more than she could. He kissed the side
of her exposed neck, savoring the taste of her. She made
a hungry little sound deep in her throat. Already tight as
a rubber band about to snap, he straightened and grabbed
her hand. "Come on," he ordered, his voice revealing the
pressure he felt. With one well-aimed kick, he sent the
kitchen door banging open.

She held back. "What are you doing? This is crazy."

"You think I don't know that?" He dragged her along
behind him, into the house and down the hall toward his
bedroom.

"We've known each other too long." She sounded desperate.

They reached his bedroom and in his eagerness, he
banged into something in the dark. Erupting into a storm
of profanity, he kicked the offending object—whatever it
was—across the room where it rattled off a wall. Two
more steps and he swung her around and unceremon-
iously tipped her over onto the bed.

"Hey!" She bounced upright, the reality of the bed pro-
viding her with unexpected strength. She reached for the
lamp on the bedside table.

Light flooded the room, illuminating Ben with his shirt
already half off. She stared at him, her question forgotten. The lamplight subtly gilded the belly ridged with
muscle and the smooth golden chest.

He ripped the shirt off and tossed it aside. His face
looked tight and flushed, the pale hair tousled. His
expression was at once intense and curiously uncertain.

But his voice sounded arrogant and sure. "I'm tired of
fooling around—I'm taking you to bed." He looked her

over with bold approval, a faint, lusty smile curving his lips. "This seemed the logical place, but if you prefer chandeliers or al fresco settings I'll try to accommodate you."

She shook her head helplessly, leaning over to cover her eyes with her hands. *What in the hell am I doing?* she asked herself. *Have I completely lost my mind?* Aloud she said, "This is beyond ridiculous. I don't want to do this."

"The hell you don't." Certainty again, and a challenge for her to deny it.

She couldn't, not in so many words. "Ben, you're rushing me." She threw back her head and glared at him. "I don't do this kind of thing."

He gave her a searching look, the lights and shadows around him emphasizing the hard strength of his face and the cleft in his chin. "Neither do I, as a rule. This is the first time since. . . ."

He didn't have to go on. She knew what he was trying to say—since his wife died. That admission splintered her resolve.

What the hell am I saving it for? she wondered suddenly. *I'm not some ingenue, I'm a mature woman. And I've been alone too long.*

What if she passed up this opportunity and never got a second chance with this man? That possibility frightened her. She reached over and curved one hand possessively across the top of his denim-covered thigh. The muscle beneath her hand bunched and he went rigid, his slitted gaze on her face asking an unspoken question.

Holding her breath, she nodded.

He smiled, and all the anger in him seemed to simply evaporate. He laced his fingers through hers and drew her to her knees on the bed. She lifted one leg and put her foot on the floor, using the leverage of his hand to stand.

A little embarrassed, she dropped her gaze. Her silk blouse hung in tatters, but she didn't care about that. She did, however, care that she was practically naked to the waist. Automatically she wrapped the fabric across her breasts. "All right," she agreed breathlessly. "But before things get completely out of control, we'd better. . . ."

He covered her hands with his and slowly drew them away. The remnants of the blouse followed. "Better what, Juli?" He leaned down and nuzzled her loose bra aside.

She gulped. "B-better be prepared." She gripped his biceps with her hands, loving the powerful feel of him. She felt the flick of his tongue against the underswell of her breast. It never occurred to her to resist when he slid the blouse and bra off her shoulders.

He sucked her nipple deep into his mouth. Her nipples had gone untouched for so long that at the first hot caress of his tongue, she gasped and her knees buckled.

He lowered her onto the bed, his mouth never leaving her. She wanted to cry, she wanted to scream. His hand stroked down her stomach, curved naturally between her legs, and she moaned. With a last mighty effort of will, she caught his head between her hands. He tilted up to look into her eyes, his own questioning.

"We need . . . something," she groaned.

"Something . . . ?" He frowned and then understood. "Oh, you mean. . . . Where's your purse?"

"It's—what's that got to do with anything?" She lifted her head off the bed to see him better, her chin on her chest and his chin between her breasts. With one hand, he continued the erotic massage between her legs, his touch burning through her slacks.

They stared into each other's eyes, the horrible truth dawning slowly. Ben pulled away abruptly and shoved his shaggy blond hair out of his eyes.

Juliana rolled over to put distance between them, then sat up, naked above the waist. "Do you mean you don't have any...?"

His expression was fierce. "The word you're searching for is 'condoms,' and that's exactly what I mean. It's been a long time since I needed one, Juliana."

"Well how did you expect us to...?" She gestured helplessly at the messy bedspread and their own state of dishabille.

"I thought *you'd* be prepared."

"I've never bought a condom in my life! At the risk of sounding old fashioned, I'm not that kind of a girl." Incensed, she sprang to her feet and yanked the bra into place. She hooked it and stared down at the remains of her blouse. "I can't leave looking like this," she said in a low, tight voice.

"You're going to *leave*? What the hell are you, a—"

"Don't say it!" She turned toward him, her face burning. She had never been so humiliated in her life. "You'll have to lend me something to wear home."

The bedsprings creaked as he stood up. He gestured with both hands. "Hey, help yourself," he said bitterly. "I'm just glad I've got *something* you want."

She wanted to tell him he had plenty she wanted, but she was too disappointed and upset to risk a verbal battle. She grabbed the first piece of clothing she saw—a chambray shirt hanging from a hook behind the door. She yanked the tails of her blouse out of her waistband and slipped out of the ruined garment, letting it fall to the floor.

She shrugged into the shirt and buttoned it up. It reached almost to her knees and she felt infinitely safer once she had it on.

He simply watched her, his face impassive but his muscles noticeably tense.

Hand on the doorknob, she paused. "I'm sorry," she said in a low, tight voice. "I . . . I don't know what happened."

"I do," he said.

Without answering, she opened the bedroom door and walked out.

As SHE TURNED into her driveway, she saw Pete's car parked in front of the house. She groaned. For a second she contemplated backing out and driving away again, but couldn't bring herself to do it. This was, after all, her home.

What a suitably miserable conclusion for a miserable drive home. She punched the remote garage opener and the door slid up smoothly; she drove inside and cut the engine. Pete walked in behind her and waited while she closed the garage door before climbing out of her car.

He wasted no time broaching the subject of his visit. "Now see here, Juliana, Paige is really upset this time and I think you're being . . ." His voice trailed off. "Jehosephat, what happened to you?"

Her face burned. "Nothing." She hurried to the inner door and unlocked it.

He followed her inside. "Are you okay? Where did you get that shirt? You look like you been spit at and hit."

"Well, I haven't!" She whirled on him, blocking the hallway. She hadn't even remembered she was wearing Ben's shirt until Pete opened his big mouth. "If you're here to criticize, you can just—"

"Simmer down, simmer down!" He held up his hands placatingly, palms forward. "I'm here to talk about Paige. Any chance I can get a beer out of you, or at least a glass of water? I've been waiting almost an hour."

"I suppose." Reluctantly she led the way to the kitchen and gestured toward the refrigerator. "Help yourself."

He did. While he extracted a can of soda and popped the top, Juliana sat down at the breakfast bar, twisting her hands together in her lap. She felt so tightly strung it scared her.

Peter took a swig from his can. "You want anything? You look like you could use a stiff belt of something."

"No," she said automatically, then reconsidered. "Yes. The white wine in the refrigerator—just dump it in a water glass."

He honored the request, but looked askance at her as he poured. "I guess Paige isn't the only one who had a bad evening." He handed her the glass, which contained at least eight ounces of wine.

"I've had better." She lifted the glass to her lips and slugged down a quarter of the contents. "I needed that," she said with heartfelt sincerity.

"I can tell."

The depth of knowledge in his piercing glance made her shift uncomfortably on her stool. He'd always known her too well. Maybe that's why she'd married him in the first place. Maybe that's why she'd divorced him, she thought with sudden insight.

She set the glass on the table. "Is Paige still mad at me?"

Pete settled his lanky form onto a stool. "She's not mad at you, Juli. She's unhappy because she's afraid you're going to fight her on this. I told her not to worry."

She gave him an exasperated look. "You couldn't speak for me when we were married, Pete. What makes you think I'll stand for it now?"

He shrugged. He didn't look upset, and in fact seemed indifferent to her growing anger. "I don't care whether you'll stand for it or not, babe. She's my daughter, too. If she wants to be a nurse, I'll figure out some way for her to get her chance."

Juliana's mouth dropped open and she stared at him. Peter had enough trouble supporting his second family, even without any financial obligation to the first. How on earth would he come up with the money to send Paige to nursing school?

Not that he'd have to. Juliana wouldn't let him even if he tried. She opened her mouth to explain that to him and instead said a single word. "Fine."

"Fine?" He frowned as if she'd finally surprised him.

"Fine," she repeated. "If that's what she truly wants, it's all right with me. Tell her so, if you want."

"Wait a minute. Is this a trick?"

She wanted to laugh, but not with Pete. "Look," she said, her voice trembling, "she can do what she likes. I've got other things on my mind."

Pete stared at her for a moment and then his dark eyes widened with understanding. "Wait a minute," he said slowly. "That shirt you're wearing... Who do I know who wears chambray shirts? Could it be you've been whiling away the hours with Mr. Benjamin Wade, gentleman avocado farmer?"

"Don't be ridiculous." She took another swallow of wine to calm herself and avoided meeting his eyes.

"It's been so long since you showed any interest in a man I was beginning to think you were going gay."

"Pete!"

"Okay, okay." He held up his hands as if in surrender, but his brown eyes sparkled with familiar mischief. "Convince me. Trot out whatever story you've concocted to throw me off the scent."

She groaned.

"C'm'on, Juliana. If it isn't Ben who's got you all worked up, then what is it?" He looked genuinely concerned, and genuinely skeptical.

"It's . . . everything." She gestured vaguely. "It's being bald—"

"You're not bald. I meant to mention how fast your hair's growing back."

"Well, I *feel* bald." Especially now—she'd forgotten to retrieve her wig. "And it's forgetting things and mixing up times and sequences and not being able to handle numbers. Pete, my attention span is about ninety seconds long." *Except when Ben put his arms around me—that improved my concentration by at least a thousand percent.*

"Ah, honey." Pete leaned across the table and patted her on the hand, his expression contrite. "You're expecting too much of yourself too fast. Lighten up, okay?"

How often had he said those words or similar ones to her? When they'd been married, he'd constantly tried to get her to lighten up—on him, on their child, on herself. Naturally, she hadn't. Now she tried to sound casual. "Pete, do you think I'm a mercenary snob?"

He considered the matter carefully, which made no brownie points with her. Finally he said, "I wouldn't necessarily choose those words. But I bet I know who did."

She felt the telltale blush rise in her cheeks, yet persisted. "Don't jump to conclusions."

"Juli, you could do worse. If Ben can't handle you, nobody can. And I oughta know."

"I don't want to be 'handled,' as you call it. I—"

The telephone rang. Wild hope flared in Juliana's breast; it had to be Ben, calling to apologize.

Calling to tell her he couldn't live through another night without her.

Calling to tell her he was on his way with a pocket full of condoms.

She glanced at Pete. "Anything else?"

"Nope, that's it. Answer the phone and I'll let myself out."

"Thanks." She didn't wait for him to go; she flew across the room and snatched the receiver off the wall. "Ben?" she cried with absolute certainty.

Silence. It stretched out, thin and endless. Then a voice said her name, questioningly... the voice of Cary Goddard.

8

JULIANA TRIED to cover her disappointment. "Cary. What a surprise."

"So I gather. You were expecting someone else?"

"Not really. Uhh—where are you?"

"Denver. I'll be flying to Miami and then on to Perth by the middle of next month."

So he wouldn't be back in Summerhill for the foreseeable future. Good, she thought. "You sound busy."

"I am." He hesitated and then added, "But that doesn't mean I've forgotten."

She felt a sudden shaft of panic. Forgotten what? Was he talking business or personal? "You haven't?"

"I want that land, Juliana, and I want that project." Cary's voice snapped across the wires, cold and final. "I don't like unfinished business. I never have."

Her hackles rose. "Ben's a stubborn man, Cary. You can't force him to sell if he doesn't want to."

"Can't I?" Cary's abrupt laugh held a cutting edge. "We'll see. As financially overextended as he is, anything's possible. I just want you to know nothing's changed. Our agreement is still in effect and I want you to reopen negotiations the first chance you get."

"Cary, I doubt Ben will—"

His nasty laugh cut her off. "Just do it." His aggressive tone softened. "And Juliana, I'm delighted with your recovery."

"Are you?" She spoke coolly, remembering his lack of attention during her hospital stay, and since.

He hesitated, then said in a rush, "The truth is, I don't handle sickness very well." He sounded uncomfortable. "I'm sorry—that's just the way I am."

"But they said you came to visit me in the hospital."

"Yeah, and it's one of the hardest things I ever did. I just want you to understand why I haven't been back. When this is all over—well, we'll see where we are. But for the time being, rest assured that our business arrangement is intact. I have every confidence that you'll find a way to convince Ware to cooperate."

Before she could respond—before she could think of a way to respond—the line went dead. Filled with foreboding, she hung up the telephone. Both her personal and professional relationships with Cary Goddard were apparently in limbo.

She poured another glass of wine and carried it into the family room. Cary's call worried her. Everything was different, now that she saw Ben's side. She wouldn't lift a finger to encourage the sale of his land—commission be damned. Which meant she had to sever all business ties with Goddard Enterprises, regardless of the buyer-broker agreement.

A chill shivered down her back. She'd worked hard to establish that business relationship, but she wouldn't reconsider—couldn't, feeling the way she did. She'd just have to return the fee Cary had already paid her. It went against her grain, but it had to be done.

Discontented, she stared at the selection of CDs and tapes and records, finally choosing one of the oldest recordings on the racks. She punched a few buttons, turned down the lights and curled up on a corner of the couch, nursing her glass of wine. The heartbreakingly bluesy sound of Billie Holiday surrounded her.

And she thought of Ben.

Ben. She groaned. Over and over, she replayed their encounter from the beginning, goose bumps prickling her arms at the erotic images flickering behind her closed eyelids. She longed for him, ached for him—damned him for forcing her to confront her own frustrations.

Why doesn't he call?

She jumped to her feet and prowled across the room, Billie's raw lament goading her. She remembered Ben's hands on her breast, Ben's lips on her throat, and the way she'd felt. . . .

Damn him! She *had* changed, whether he believed her or not. She knew what counted and what didn't. It's just that sometimes she found it hard to remember under the stress of the moment.

But that's all right, she reassured herself. *I'm alive, and while I am, there's a chance to make everything right.*

She'd smell the damned roses or know the reason why!

She stopped stock-still, the empty wineglass in her hand. She wanted a cigarette. No use looking for one, though. She'd turned the house inside out in that same futile search at least five times since her release from the hospital. Each time Ben had provided the moral support she needed to resist temptation.

This time Ben was more tempting than the temptation, so she couldn't look for strength there. Ben, always Ben...she shivered and hugged her arms across her chest, remembering the way his hands stroked her, the way her body melted into his.

All those years, and she'd never really looked at him...at those blue eyes, so alert and intelligent, the high wide cheekbones and strong, masculine jaw that so enthralled her now.

She had always rather approved of the slight cleft in his chin, but now she thought also of the deeply chiseled lines framing his mouth. And the mouth itself, with lips that looked so hard but felt so soft, especially when they parted and she could feel the flick of his tongue against her flesh....

She shuddered and opened her eyes. She couldn't believe what she was feeling—she was standing alone in the middle of her own home, drinking wine and hallucinating and getting hotter and hotter.

Her glass was empty. She could drink more wine and most likely get quietly and completely soused, or she could...go to the store, buy a pack of cigarettes and smoke the damned things.

She grabbed a scarf and left the wineglass on the wet bar on her way out.

SHE WALKED into the all-night grocery store, straight to the tobacco section and right on past. Up one aisle and down the other she marched with determined stride, until finally she found what she sought, between the sanitary napkins and the paper plates.

She had never dreamed there were so many different kinds and brands of condoms in the entire world. She swallowed hard and clenched her jaw until it ached. She resisted the guilty urge to glance around, certain that if she did, she'd see someone she knew. Some things it was better not to know.

What the hell? One kind was probably as good as the next. She grabbed the nearest box—a variety pack, for heaven's sake. *Variety is the spice of life*, she reminded herself, hope springing eternal.

She picked up a box of tissues and a roll of trash bags as she headed for the checkout counter, just to keep her variety pack from rattling around on the conveyer belt all by its lonesome.

BEN HEARD the sound of the car's engine and walked out of the barn to watch the Mercedes draw to a stop. Juliana climbed out and paused beside the car, looking at the house.

He called her name softly and it seemed to hover in the hushed night air. She turned, her motions jerky. For a moment they stared at each other across the moonlit expanse and then they were running, into each other's arms.

"I'm sorry," she murmured. "I'm sorry, Ben. I've been an idiot—"

"Shh—it's all right. You're here now." He kissed her up-turned face, his hands roaming freely over her back and sides. In the silvery moonlight, he saw her eyelids drift closed.

She turned her face toward him blindly and he kissed her, at last giving free rein to all the pent-up longing. His hands, made clumsy by haste, tightened on her waist and dragged her body hard against his. His tongue probed aggressively, then plunged inside her mouth in one swift joining thrust.

He slid his hands up over her ribs, beneath the too-big chambray shirt. She pressed closer, adjusting her hips to his, and his body tightened in response.

He jerked his head back, breathing hard. By the light of a full moon and a million stars, he looked down at her.

Her fingers dug into his shoulders. "What is it? Ben, we don't have to stop. I brought . . . condoms."

He felt a silly grin stretch his lips; even now, she found it difficult to say the word. But there was one more hurdle to clear. "Are you sure this is okay, Juli? I mean, what we're about to do?"

She stroked his jaw with fingers that trembled. One corner of her soft mouth curved up. "What is it we're about to do, Ben?" Her warm voice teased him. "There's a name for it, as I'm sure you know."

"There are a lot of names for it, but the variation I have in mind is called making love." His voice felt like a growl ripped from somewhere deep within his chest. If he were a lion, he thought, he'd be roaring.

To Juliana, he *was* a lion, a great tawny beast who could devour her or fill her with joy on a whim. She felt vulnerable and exposed, but also excited and eager. To her amazement, she found she trusted him enough to violate one of her cardinal rules—enough to take a chance.

"You haven't answered me, Juli. You haven't been out of the hospital all that long. Are there any medical reasons we shouldn't—" his voice dropped to velvet depths "—make love?"

She caught her breath. "No."

"Did you ask the doctor? Specifically?" He pulled her into his arms, settling his chin over the top of her head.

"Of course not." She found breathing increasingly difficult. "I never expected the situation to arise. Besides, it was my brain they operated on, not my—"

He let out a whoop of laughter. "Your what?"

She felt her cheeks grow hot. "Never mind that. The doctor said I could get married. I figure that included clearance for the honeymoon."

"Married!" He went very still. After a moment, his chest shook with suppressed laughter. "Uh-oh, you know about the great engagement hoax."

"Yes." She could barely speak as he slowly slid one hand down to cover her hip, his fingers kneading gently. He kissed her ear, then tickled it with his tongue until she gasped and clung to him.

His voice sounded warmly intimate. "And you forgive me for lying?"

She groaned. "What do you think?"

"I think it's time we continued this discussion elsewhere." He swung her around toward the house and clamped her to his side with one arm. "Let's go inside."

"O-okay."

He must have heard something in that single word because he stopped and pulled her fully into his arms again. "What is it, baby?" His smoky voice cajoled her to answer.

"Nothing," she denied too quickly. She buried her face in the crook of his neck.

"Don't hold out on me." He kissed the top of her head, nuzzling the short silky hair.

"No, really. I just feel incredibly stupid admitting... admitting that—"

After a moment's silence, he said gently, "You're embarrassed, right?"

Her cheeks burned. "How did you guess?"

His arms tightened around her. "I didn't guess. I feel the same way."

"You're kidding!" Nervous laughter bubbled in her throat and she choked it back. "What's wrong with us, Ben? At our age... and we've known each other practically all our lives."

"Nothing's wrong with us." He stroked the side of her face. "Sure, we go back a long way, but that has nothing to do with it. It's much simpler—you're a one-man woman and I'm a one-woman man. We don't take a roll in the hay lightly."

"I was beginning to think I was a no-man woman," she admitted wryly, to cover up the thrill of pleasure his words gave her.

"I am about to put that fear to rest forever." He grabbed her hand and whirled away from the house, tugging her along. "Speaking of a roll in the hay—"

"Where are we going?" She broke into a reluctant trot in the effort to keep pace.

"I'm making it easier."

"But—"

"No buts. Trust me. Didn't you ever fantasize about making love in a hayloft?"

"Sure—when I was about sixteen!" Laughing and breathless, she allowed him to pull her inside the inky interior of the barn. With a minimum of groping and miscues, he guided her to the ladder leading to the hayloft, set her feet upon it and gave her a pat, which more closely resembled a caress, on the bottom.

Excited and intrigued, she scrambled up. He followed and at the top, caught her in his arms.

"I sleep up here sometimes," he explained, turning her in his embrace so she could see silver moonlight spilling through the open loft doors at each end. "And this isn't hay, its straw. You'd have to be a masochist to sleep on hay."

"I might be willing to try, if that's the only way I could...." She choked on the words.

"Say it." His hands massaged her arms, raising goose flesh. "Say anything you want."

She drew in a shaky breath. "If that's the only way I could have you, Ben. The way I feel right now, I could lie on a bed of spikes or walk barefoot through hot coals. I don't know what's happening to me."

She clutched the hem of the too-big shirt and drew it smoothly over her head and tossed it aside, without bothering with a single button. "All I know is that I'm mad for you."

He reached around behind her and unsnapped her bra. He kissed the curve of her shoulder while he slipped the straps from her shoulders and let the whole fall to the floor. Her trembling fingers fumbled with the waistband of her slacks, and then she was naked and eager for him.

Sighing with pleasure, she pressed her breasts against him, rubbing her nipples into the smoothly muscled expanse of his bare chest. His hands on her shoulder blades traced erotic circles, making her arch against him.

She tugged impatiently at the snap of his jeans. "Come *on*. What are you waiting for?"

His low, languid laughter skittered along her nerve endings. "You're a greedy little thing, once you make up your mind."

"I know."

She ran her hands up and down his rib cage with reckless abandon, only his quickened breathing betraying his excitement. But she knew. Her palms skimmed across his chest; her fingertips flicked over his flat nipples and she heard the quick hiss of his breath.

"Juli." Her name was a guttural moan on his lips.

He scooped her up in his arms and strode to one end of the hayloft. Bending, he deposited her on a pile of straw covered with blankets . . . quilts—she didn't take time to make the distinction. She just lay there and watched him throw off his clothing.

Moonlight made him a work of art, gilding a body honed down to magnificent essentials. No fat showed on belly or flanks, and his smooth, well-defined muscles flexed with his hurried movements. She stared at the denseness of his man's body, and all the passion she had denied so vehemently surged up into her throat, strong enough to choke her.

In exquisite anticipation, she lifted her arms to him, tinder awaiting his match.

BEN STOOD OVER the pallet, gazing down at the woman who had somehow managed to make him feel whole again. Juliana, of all people—who said life wasn't funny?

He dropped to his knees and sat back on his heels, his hands resting on his bare thighs. He just wanted to look at her for a moment, savor the gifts she brought him.

"W-what is it, Ben?"

He could hear her teeth chatter around the words, and not from cold, he realized. He reached out to touch the gentle curve of her hip and she caught her breath. "You're beautiful," he said thickly. "I always thought so."

"Did you?"

He heard the pleasure in her voice. He slid his hand up over her rib cage and covered her breast, gently squeezing. She drew in her breath in a little gasp, but didn't move. In the silvery light, he saw her lick her lips.

He bent to her mouth and she rose to meet him, tangling her hands in his hair to pull him closer. Kiss for kiss she matched him, her mouth hot and wet and sweet with passion.

He could barely control his craving for her; he wanted to take her quickly and ruthlessly. He'd meant it when he called himself a one-woman man. His commitments, once made, were strong.

He parted her thighs and covered the springy curling hair at the base of her belly with his palm. With mounting urgency, he moved his hand in a subtle rhythm, rubbing and coaxing her. She responded perfectly as if they'd done this a thousand times, and his fingers began to delve more deeply into the torrid heat of her.

He felt her response build, first in a soft gasp lost in his mouth, then in the tightening of her muscles. She clutched at his shoulders, nails biting with sharp-sweet pain into his skin.

"Now," she whispered raggedly, her arms suddenly urging him up. "Please!"

He turned away for the instant needed to prepare and then he rolled over her, his knees between her parted legs and his hands above her shoulders. Shuddering, he looked down at her. Her eyes were closed and her head strained back on her slender throat. Her breath came in urgent little gasps and her entire body trembled.

For an instant he held himself poised there. Her eyes opened unexpectedly, dark pools in her strained face, and she reached for him.

He entered her with a single lightning stroke. Slick and ready, she yielded to him, rising to meet the joining thrust. Her strangled cry urged him on.

His new hardness moved inside her and she moaned a little. Rotating her hips, she wrapped her legs high and tight around his torso.

Gasping, he tried to control the pace. Sheathed as he was in her fiery depths, he felt himself nearing the edge too soon. Tension gathered and built in his straining muscles with every fierce stroke.

She clawed at his shoulders, bucking her hips beneath his. Consciously or not, her tight hot sheath convulsed around his hard length and he jackknifed, control stripped away in an instant. She urged him on with soft cries of passion and he responded, his powerful strokes ramming into her enveloping softness with increasing force.

She writhed beneath him, her murmured endearments inciting him to penetrate to the very limit of his ability to give—and hers to receive. He felt her first tiny contraction begin, begin and grow into deep, deep convulsions that consumed her entire body. She cried out, a strangled wail that ended on a note so intense it might have been agony but wasn't.

That did it—he arched above her, his head flung back at the final stroke. Somehow her ecstasy was his and they were one. Exploding into the release he had initiated, he pitched forward into the maelstrom.

THEY LAY SIDE BY SIDE on the pallet on the straw, their breathing almost, but not quite, returned to normal. She turned her head to the side to smile at him. He looked like she felt—limp, exhausted . . . and replete.

She rolled over and snuggled closer to his side. The movement put her on some kind of lump. She shifted and reached beneath her to smooth away the obstruction and realized she'd found the box of condoms. Smiling, she rubbed a hand across his broad chest. His skin felt warm and silky beneath her palm.

"Are you cold?" His husky voice startled her.

"No. Oh, no."

He hauled her more snugly against his side. "You shivered."

"But not from cold." She kissed his shoulder, wishing she knew how to tell him how she felt. "I can't believe what just happened," she said finally. "To me, of all people!"

His hand stroked her short hair. "Yeah. The tough cookie just crumbled."

"The not-so-tough cookie, as it turns out." She bit her lip. "Ben, do you realize that if I hadn't nearly died, we wouldn't be here like this?"

He grew very still. "You can't be sure. We might have found each other, somehow."

She knew that wasn't true, and she didn't think he believed it, either. There was no way she'd have let herself open up to him, had it not been through necessity. It had taken a catastrophic illness to tear down her carefully constructed defenses.

And his feelings toward her hadn't exactly been friendly at the start, either. They wanted different things. He wanted to keep his land, she wanted to be instrumental in its sale.

As he'd said, life was completely at the mercy of "ifs," she thought. If she hadn't gotten sick . . . if he hadn't saved her life . . . if, if, if.

She flexed her body into his and sighed. There'd be plenty of time for introspection later on. At the moment, she felt wonderful, adrift on a soft cloud of sensual satisfaction more complete than any she could have conjured up.

Elaborately casual, she rubbed her hand down his chest, over his navel and lower. He tensed, but not in displeasure, and she knew he was trying to ignore the tugging of her fingers as they walked their way closer to danger.

Her fingers settled over the core of him, velvet stretched over resurgent flesh that bloomed beneath her touch. Warming to her task, she was completely unprepared for the brush of something furry and alive against the soles of her feet.

She screamed and bolted up, her hand tightening convulsively around his most sensitive appendage.

"Take it easy!" he roared, his own hand flying to cover hers. "You trying to make me a soprano?"

"Good lord, no!" She loosened her hold on him, realizing that Freeloader was the intruder. "It's that damned

cat!" Her heart raced in the aftermath of panic. The kitten
purred from somewhere deep in the shadows, no longer a
threat. She shivered and turned contritely back toward
Ben. "Did I hurt you?"

Ostensibly to make amends, she began to stroke him
softly, but not soothingly. She felt his instant response.
With a strangled groan, he fell back on the blanket and
submitted to her determined fingers.

"You know," she said conversationally, rolling over to
crouch between his parted thighs, "I'd be interested to
know where you got that condom, since the ones I bought
are still in my purse which is still in my car." She ripped
open a little foil packet and fumbled for the contents.

"Actually—" He swallowed hard and his body rocked
convulsively. He seemed to choke on the words. "As soon
as you left, I made a little trip to town myself."

Her hand tightened dangerously over the shaft of flesh
and she leaned down until her lips touched his corded
belly. "You were that sure of me?"

"I was sure—" he gasped "—that if you didn't come
back, I'd go get you."

And then he did just that.

LATER, THE NIGHT CHILL sent them trooping down the
ladder and into the house. Laughing, touching, they carried with them such items of clothing as they found in the
dark—a shoe, a pair of Levi's, a bra.

Dizzy with happiness, Juliana drifted naked through the
silvery moon-washed night. As if in a dream, she held out
her hand to Ben and he took it, his touch warm and real.

"I wish I could tell you how I feel," he blurted, his naturally gravelly voice even more hoarse than usual.

"You do. Oh, you do." Holding his hand, she spiraled
toward him, laughing, wrapping his arm around her as she

moved. Their naked bodies met and he held her tight and kissed her—a long, intoxicating exploration.

They entered the house through the kitchen door, stumbling around in the dark, laughing, whispering, holding each other. It took a long time to make it as far as the bedroom, but she, drunk with pleasure, minded not at all.

Once in his room, he switched on the light and scooped her up into his arms. Dropping her onto the bed, he grinned down at her—the grin fading into a concerned frown. He knelt beside the bed and with one forefinger, traced the purple-pink scar on her stomach.

"Does it hurt?" he asked.

"No." She lay still, letting him examine the scar. "I don't even remember when they did it, only what I was told later."

"*I* remember." He shuddered and a muscle leaped in his jaw. His hand curved over the scar, covering it. "I thought you were going to die."

"But I didn't. Thanks to you, I didn't."

He closed his eyes, but not before she saw the pain and uncertainty in them. Tears stung her own eyes and she blinked away the moisture. She had difficulty keeping her voice steady enough to speak. "Thanks to you, my entire life has changed. Being here like this is . . . is a dream." She reached up to cup his face with her hands. "A dream I didn't even know I had—I guess all along I wanted you and not a cigarette."

He growled deep in his throat. "Kind'a blows you away to think about it, doesn't it."

"Umm."

He slid one hand down her flat belly to tangle in the thicket of hair at the juncture of her thighs. She caught her breath in a hiss. "Stop that, Ben. I've got to get up and go home. You're not making it easy."

He coaxed her with rhythmic movements of his hand. "You don't want to go home and I'm not interested in making it easy."

"Of course, I don't *want* to go home but—" She felt the delicacy of his touch where she most wanted it and choked.

"Then again, maybe you're right." Slowly... reluctantly... teasingly he slid his hand away, over her belly, up to cover a breast. "It must be 2:00 or 3:00 a.m. already and one of us has to go to work tomorrow."

"What are you talking about?" With her hands she urged him up and into the bed with her, wrapping her arms and legs around him. "I don't..." Only she did. Dismayed, she remembered the Burtons and groaned. "Wait a minute. That was Opal's idea. I never agreed to anything."

"But you will."

He slipped his hand back into the notch between her thighs and stroked up, moving his fingers higher and deeper. Her muscles began to tremble and she closed her eyes.

"I guess you're right." Her voice faded as tension mounted. At the first blunt probing of his finger, her concentration splintered entirely and a long drawn-out "ahh" escaped her taut throat.

She didn't want to think about tomorrow. Tomorrow would bring reality crashing back around her ears, whatever that reality might be. But for once, she found herself willing—no, eager—to take a chance.

He eased a finger inside and she rose to meet his hand, moving slowly, languorously, his mastery causing undulating waves to ripple clear to the soles of her feet. He caught her nipple lightly between his teeth and tugged, gently insistent. Ecstatic, she arched her back.

He rolled over her, his knees sliding between her thighs, his breathing heavy. She trembled beneath him, hot and slick and eager to receive him. Eager to be his.

Suddenly emotion welled up in her chest, choking her. She had never felt so close to another human being, not even her husband. Not even in the first days of their marriage when she swore she'd love him forever.

Ben lowered himself slowly, probing, and she took him in, drew him in gladly, her hips surging to meet his.

"Ben—" She gasped as he reached full penetration and sank against her with an explosive sigh.

He groaned, his face pressed against her throat. "You want to talk *now*?"

"N-no." She swallowed hard and began to undulate her hips, creating a sweet friction. "I . . . I just wanted to say that . . . maybe . . ."

He raised up on his elbows, jamming his hips down against hers, filling her perfectly and completely. "Could you talk a little faster? I'm about to go out of my mind, here."

"I think . . . I think I love you." She stared at him, horrified, afraid he'd laugh, or worse—only what could be worse?

He wasn't laughing. His eyes narrowed and he glared down at her, even as his rigid flesh stirred to new life inside her.

"You don't *think* you love me," he rasped out, beginning a rhythmic advance and retreat. "You damned well *know* you love me. Otherwise you wouldn't be *here* . . ." He jammed into her almost violently and she felt the delicious shivers begin deep inside, where their bodies joined. "Doing *this*...." Another thrust, deep and swift and sure. "With *me!*"

He shuddered and she felt the spasm overtake him and radiate out into her own body, hotter and brighter than anything she had ever known. As the most exquisite convulsions carried her away, she knew it was true.

She did love him—oh, she loved him!

9

JULIANA AWOKE to a brand new world, a world brimming with promise. If she could still feel this way in the sober light of day, then anything was possible, she told herself as she shared morning coffee with Ben. She didn't want to eat; she just wanted to look, to touch, to be with him.

But of course, she couldn't. She couldn't afford to surrender her independence. She'd pull back for a couple of days, then reassess the situation.

"Will I see you tonight?" he asked as she prepared to leave.

She looked at him, at the hard handsome face and the body that delivered on all its promises, and she wanted to say yes. Instead she hedged. "I'm not sure. It depends on how things go in the office, and with Paige."

"Hmm," he said. "A definite maybe."

She wished he'd been more upset by her lack of decisiveness, but he just shrugged.

She drove home, showered, dressed in a business suit and headed out again. She had one stop to make before meeting the Burtons.

The tantalizing aroma of tomatoes and garlic and cheese surrounded her with a new intensity as she walked into Señor Pizza. It seemed as if everything in her life had become more intense, more real. She felt like a kid—a teenager in love. Only, when she'd actually *been* a teenager in love, it was a pale imitation of this.

She spotted Pete behind the counter, tossing a circle of pizza dough into the air and catching it on an extended fist. Gradually he spun it larger and larger. Several young employees worked beside him, loading meat and vegetables and cheese onto the dough and shoving pizzas into the revolving oven.

Pete looked surprised to see her there. While he stared, the circle of dough sailed past his extended fist and plopped onto the wooden work table.

He dismissed the lump of dough without so much as a glance and walked toward the counter. "What's with you?" he demanded suspiciously. "You look like the cat that got the cream."

She laughed, because that's just how she felt—and not because of the makeup or the new clothes or the wig, rescued from the grass outside Ben's kitchen door.

"Thanks. I think." She dropped her glance, fighting the silly smile tugging at the corners of her mouth.

"Hell of a turnaround since I left you last night." He cocked his head to one side, his eyes narrowing.

A young employee tried to edge past the boss to reach the cash register. "Excuse me, Pete."

Pete stepped aside and nodded at Juliana. "Is it safe to assume you didn't drop by for lunch?"

"Good guess."

"In that case, come on back to the office."

He led her through the storeroom and on to the curtained cubbyhole that served as the nerve center of his pizza operation. He waved her toward the only chair but she shook her head.

"I'm not staying. I just came to give you this." She opened her purse and took out a check. "Call it a loan, call it a gift, whatever you like."

Pete took the check slowly. He looked at the slip of paper, blinked and looked again. "Ten thousand dollars?" He sounded as if he doubted his eyesight.

She shifted uncomfortably. "That's the amount you need, isn't it?"

"Yes."

That familiar feeling of missing the obvious settled over her. "Then what's the matter?"

His lips tightened. "You already turned me down once. I've never known you to change your mind after it's made up. What's going on, Juliana?"

Honesty was difficult. "I don't remember, Pete. When did we talk about it?"

"The day you got sick—actually, just before it happened. At Ben's." His eyes widened with sudden understanding and he struck himself on the forehead with an open palm. "I get it. You don't remember because of the aneurysm."

She nodded. "There's a lot I've forgotten."

"In this case, I can only be glad. Unless you want to take it back, now that you know?" He looked hungrily at the check.

"The money's yours, Pete. I owe you that and more."

He let out a long, low whistle. "You really *have* changed." He grinned. "I don't know how I'll ever thank you, honey."

He hadn't called her "honey" in a long, long time. Her eyes burned and she swallowed back the lump in her throat, flustered but strangely gratified. Impulsively she reached out and squeezed his hand. "Don't worry, I'll think of something," she said, trying to cover her embarrassment. "I just hope this will make a difference for you."

"And how." He folded the check and tucked it into his chest pocket. He took her arm and guided her out of the office. "I don't know what happened to you last night but—wait a minute."

He stopped in the middle of the store room, between boxes of napkins and giant cans of black olives. "Maybe I *do* know."

She blushed. She felt it, an actual blush. He took one look at the red tide rising over her cheeks and burst out laughing. She bit her lip and looked away.

"You and Ben," he said, his tone heavy with amazement. "Damn, who'd have thought it?"

She started to deny everything, but caught herself in time. She had nothing to be ashamed of. "Do you think I've lost my mind?" she asked with a wry laugh.

"You? No. Ben? Maybe." He shook his head wonderingly.

"Then you really don't mind—your ex-wife and your friend?"

"Why should I? Did you mind when I married Sandra?"

"I was glad," she admitted. "It made me feel a little less guilty."

"Wow, you really are a new woman." They turned back toward the doorway and he put an arm around her shoulder, the way he used to do before things went bad. "This is the first time I've heard you accept even a shred of responsibility for what happened to us."

They halted at the outer door. She didn't want to meet his level gaze, but she forced herself to do so. Whatever he said to her, she owed it to him to listen.

But being Pete, good old easy-going Pete, he just smiled. "Good luck, Juliana," he said simply. "Ben's a great guy, but he's already been through a lot. You could do him some real damage if you're not careful."

Well, what about me? she thought. *I'm not made of iron.* "That sword cuts two ways, Pete."

He seemed to consider for a moment. He grinned. "Naw, not you," he scoffed. He shook his head decisively and opened the door for her.

She left feeling considerably less optimistic than when she'd arrived.

SHE WALKED IN on a party in progress at the Summerhill Real Estate Company. Nothing wild, just a half-dozen people clustered around a cake, laughing and passing around paper plates and plastic forks.

Stella saw Juliana first. "Hey, everybody, the boss is back!"

The conversational buzz halted mid-syllable and all eyes turned toward Juliana. *Good grief, what do they expect me to do? Clear the office because they're eating cake?* she wondered. That's what it looked like; expressions ranged from cautious to dismayed.

"Please," she said with a wave of her hand, "don't let me disturb the party. What's the occasion?"

An almost audible sigh of relief greeted her inquiry and everyone seemed to relax at least a degree.

"Charlie got married last weekend in Las Vegas." Stella indicated the middle-aged man in a checkered jacket.

It took Juliana a minute to even recognize Charlie Gresham. Then she did, but couldn't remember for the life of her when he'd become associated with Summerhill Realty. Nevertheless, she smiled and accepted the hand he thrust toward her. "Congratulations," she said.

Stella picked up the cake knife. "He brought in the cake to celebrate."

Charlie snickered. "And because the new Mrs. Gresham is Monica Martin of the Bread 'n' Stuff Bakery Martins."

He puffed out his chest importantly. "About all this—" A wave of his arm indicated the party fixings. "They tell me you don't like this kind of thing in the office, but I figured it'd be okay for a special occasion."

And you also figured I'd never know about it, Juliana thought. She smiled. "I don't want this office to turn into Disneyland South, but anything short of that is fine with me. I've decided it's time to stop and smell the roses." She winked at Stella, who stared with mouth agape. "And it's also time to stop and eat a piece of wedding cake."

Amidst spontaneous applause, Stella presented Juliana with an enormous chunk of cake topped by a profusion of pastel roses. After a few bites, she excused herself and carried her briefcase into her office.

Stella followed. "Sorry about that, but Charlie's not an easy man to stop. Why didn't you tell me you were coming in?" She lifted a forkful of cake to her mouth.

"It was sort of a last minute decision." True. A decision made after a night with Ben Ware. There was damned little Juliana would—or could—refuse him. Her satisfied smile slipped at the sight of paper overflowing her "in" basket. "Actually, I have an appointment in a few minutes. Opal Rudnick arranged it—a couple named Burton."

"Juliana!"

Juliana's head snapped around at her secretary's tone of alarm.

Stella rolled the now-empty paper plate into a cylinder. "The Burtons, Helen and Rodney?"

"That's right. What's the matter, Stella?"

Stella groaned. "The Burtons have been through every real-estate office in this town. No one can please them— no one can help them. Why, they even *sued* Tom Shanks."

Try as she might, Juliana couldn't conjure up any recollection of the Burtons. Her stomach clenched—just what she needed on her first day back. "This lawsuit . . . I guess that came up while I was in the hospital?"

Stella started to speak, then stopped abruptly. Her expression softened. "You really don't remember, do you? It happened almost a year ago, but never mind that. We'll just get you out of it. I'll ask John to handle them."

"No, Stella." Juliana took a determined breath. "I'll handle the Burtons."

Stella frowned. "Why on earth put yourself through that grief?"

Because I promised the man I love, Juliana reminded herself. But what she said was, "Somebody's got to do it. Why not me?"

RODNEY BURTON banged his cane down on the floor, his bushy white eyebrows drawing together above dark, hawkish eyes that denied his advanced years. "Balderdash, young woman! Balderdash! That's what I said to Mrs. Cloyd Rudnick when she told me she had arranged this meeting."

Helen Burton fluttered at her husband's side, tugging at his elbow with an ineffectual hand. He towered above her matronly five-foot frame, although he couldn't be much taller than Juliana, if any.

"Rodney, be calm, dear. You know what the doctor said." Mrs. Burton shot an apologetic glance at Juliana.

Rodney, his thin figure erect as a toy soldier's, banged the cane against the leg of a chair. "That quack!"

Juliana tried not to let her dismay show. The Burtons looked to be in their eighties, and although both appeared in possession of their faculties, Mr. Burton gave new meaning to the word *irascible*.

"Will you have a seat, Mr. and Mrs. Burton? Mrs. Rudnick didn't tell me much about your situation, so perhaps you could fill me in." The telephone rang. "If you'll just excuse me for a moment—"

Mr. Burton banged his cane against a waste-paper basket and glared at his wife. "I don't have to come here to be insulted," he boomed.

Absolutely certain that was true, Juliana gave them an apologetic smile and picked up the receiver. "Stella, I thought I asked you not to disturb us?"

"You did, but this is an emergency. Barbara Snell's on the other line. She's been trying to reach you since yesterday. Says it's important."

"Ask her to come on over. I'll be with her just as soon as I finish with Mr. and Mrs. Burton."

"Or as soon as they finish you," Stella muttered.

"Right." Juliana hung up the receiver and smiled cautiously at the couple seated before the desk. "Now, if you'll tell me your problem, we'll see if I can help you."

"By gad, madam, your veracity is at stake here." Mr. Burton whipped the tip of his cane against the desk with lightninglike speed. The burled wooden staff shattered with a sharp crack and all three jumped, then stared at the jagged edges.

In the suddenly strained silence, Helen Burton's soft voice rang clear as a bell, "Well, thank heavens! I've been waiting twenty years for that to happen!"

"AND THEN Mr. Burton looked at me, and he looked down at the cane, and he looked at Mrs. Burton, and he said, 'Helen, what are you trying to tell me?'"

Juliana collapsed with laughter, falling back against the plush desk chair. Barbara, seated across the broad expanse of mahogany, responded with a strained smile.

Juliana wiped tears from her eyes. "After that Mr. Burton was a changed man. Every time he'd start to get excited, Mrs. Burton would give that broken cane a significant look and he'd straighten right up."

"This doesn't exactly sound like your cup of tea."

Juliana overlooked the other woman's critical tone and spoke mildly. "Too true. I'm not even entirely sure what they want."

"You'll find out, soon enough. Everybody wants something."

Juliana had never heard that chilly note in Barbara's voice before, lacking even a trace of the little-girl phoniness. "I'm sorry. You're here on business. What can I do for you?"

Barbara's lips thinned and her eyes narrowed. "You can clear up a nasty rumor."

Juliana caught her breath. Surely the word wasn't already out about her and Ben. But that was ridiculous—even if anyone had heard, it couldn't exactly be classified as a "nasty rumor." She shook off her momentary dismay. "Sure," she said. "What have you heard?"

"That the Holmes property is about to sell for a hundred thousand dollars."

"The what?"

Barbara gave an inelegant snort. "Don't be coy. I'm talking about Edna and Henry Holmes—or I should say, Edna Holmes, now that Henry's dead. On Orange Tree Terrace?"

"Oh, sure." Juliana knew the property—an old falling-down frame house, but valuable land in a good area. "A hundred thousand? Boy, that's dirt cheap around there. What's the deal?"

"You ought to know. Charlie Gresham is the agent and you're his broker." Barbara clutched her purse and stood up. Her voice rang with self-righteous indignation. "I've known you a long time, Juliana, and nothing you do should surprise me. You've stolen clients from me, you've stolen listings from me, and you've lied to me. But I didn't think even *you* would stoop low enough to steal from a seventy-five year old widow."

"What are you talking about?" Aghast, Juliana stared at the other woman.

"Charlie Gresham is a sleeze and you knew it when you let him come in here. He's convinced that poor confused old lady that he's got her the deal of the century and it's at least fifty thousand less than it should be. And just guess who the buyer is?"

"Why, I don't—"

"Charlie's brother!"

"Wait a minute, wait a minute." Juliana held up her hands in appeal. "You must be mistaken. Who told you all this?"

"*She* did!" Barbara's outrage knew no bounds; she literally quivered with it. "Mrs. Holmes was sitting next to me at the Hair Today Boutique yesterday and I overheard her talking to the beautician. Poor old lady thinks Charlie can walk on water, but *some* of us know different, don't we?"

Barbara took a stiff step toward the door. "I know you're disappointed that you're out of the running for the Real Estate Star award, but your office is still in the picture for most transactions. Well, Juliana Robinson, this isn't a transaction." Barbara took a deep breath, her nostrils flaring. "*This*," she announced in ringing tones, "is *doing deals*. Your father must be turning over in his grave!"

Juliana felt as if she'd tumbled into a nightmare. She sat at her desk, her heart pounding painfully and her mind whirling as Barbara stalked to the door. She tossed a last outraged glance over her shoulder and made her exit in a huff, slamming the door.

Seconds later Stella opened the door and stuck her head inside. "What's the matter with Babs?" she asked.

"Stella, do you know anything about Charlie Gresham and an offer or a listing on the Holmes property?"

"Sure." Stella approached the desk. "Don't you remember?"

Juliana felt sick to her stomach. Apparently she had condoned Charlie's bid to take advantage of the widow Holmes. "Is Charlie out there now?"

Stella nodded. "He's about to write the contract for that deal, Juliana."

"That's what he thinks." Juliana clenched her teeth and braced her hands on the arms of her chair. "Ask Mr. Gresham to come in here, please."

SHE TRIED to couch her questions to Charlie in as unthreatening a manner as possible, but he wasn't buying it. The burly agent fidgeted while he heard her out and then exploded.

"Damn it to hell, you knew what was going on as well as I did," he shouted, jumping to his feet. His blue and green checkered jacket flapped around his ample middle as he paced the floor in front of her desk. "You're in this for the bucks, same as I am, and you take 'em where you can find 'em. Don't pull any sanctimonious B.S. on me at this late date."

Juliana pressed the heels of her palms to her throbbing head. "Goodbye, Charlie," she said, astonished to hear her voice come out strong and steady. "Our association is at an end."

"Oh, yeah?" He leaned across the desk, bracing his hands on the polished wood. "You're the one told us to pull out all the stops so we won't be standing there with egg on our faces at awards time. Besides, I just got married and I can't afford to let any live ones get away. We'll see—"

The telephone's ring intruded and Juliana grabbed for the receiver.

"It's Ben Ware," Stella announced.

Relief flooded through Juliana. "Oh, yes, put him on."

"No, I mean he's here."

The door opened simultaneously with Stella's words and Ben stood there, a question on his face. He wore the omnipresent Levi's and a white T-shirt that strained to cover his broad shoulders and powerful torso. His smile faded as he took in the scene before him.

Juliana drew strength from the very sight of him. She swung her gaze back to Charlie. "I *said* goodbye."

Charlie thrust out his fleshy lower lip and for a moment it looked as if he'd resume the argument. But Ben walked forward to stand beside Juliana, his eyes chips of blue ice. The odds had suddenly changed, along with Charlie's expectations, apparently. He straightened, his lip curling.

Ben cleared his throat, an ominous sound in the hushed room. Without another word, Charlie pivoted toward the door.

Juliana held herself stiffly erect while he stalked from the room. As the door closed, she collapsed into Ben's arms, hanging on tight.

He stroked her hair with one hand. "Easy, honey. Want to tell me what that was all about?"

"Yes." She gulped a deep breath and straightened. "Only later, okay? I have to sort this out in my mind first."

"Whatever you say." He gazed at her, his expression solemn. "I missed you. Do you mind me dropping in like this?"

"No. Oh, no!" She rose on tiptoe and brushed a light kiss across his mouth. "I was never so glad to see anyone in my life."

He caught her chin with tender fingers. "Me, neither," he said. "Any chance I'll see you tonight? This time I'm looking for the definitive answer."

"About the same as the chance the sun'll set in the west."

And when he kissed her, the chances seemed even better than that.

JULIANA WALKED into her kitchen to find Paige opening a diet soda. She looked up and grinned as if there'd never been a cross word between them. "So you went back to the office today. Good for you."

"I went back, but it wasn't all that good." Juliana opened the refrigerator and peered inside.

Paige nodded. "Okay, that takes care of your day. Now let's talk about your night."

Juliana pulled out a pitcher of orange juice and closed the refrigerator door. "Whatever do you mean?" she asked primly.

"Give me a break, Mom. I know you spent the night with Ben."

Juliana's jaw dropped and she stared at her daughter, shocked to the core. "W-why I . . . it . . . you don't . . . uhh, we—"

Paige laughed. "Don't look so shocked, Mother. I think it's great. I think *he's* great. If you want to marry him, you have my permission."

"Marry! Nobody's talking marry. Where on earth do you get these ideas?" The very word flustered Juliana, who scarcely needed any more jolts. Moving jerkily, she pulled down a juice glass from a shelf.

Paige winked broadly. "I understand," she said solemnly. "Are you going to move in with him or is he moving in here?"

"Are you crazy?" Juliana splashed juice over the rim of the glass. "Nobody's moving anywhere." And then she saw her daughter's face and realized the little brat was teasing. She'd fallen for it. Was that a guilty conscience or what? "Paige, let's be serious for a minute."

Instantly alert, the girl's expression became guarded and a little remote. "Do we have to? I have a date in a few minutes."

"You know we do. About last night . . ." Juliana finally said what she'd been steeling herself to say all day long. "I was wrong. I reacted out of habit. If you really, truly, want to be a nurse—" she swallowed hard and forced herself to total capitulation "—I'll support you all the way."

"Do you mean it?" Paige gave her mother a wary look. "That's almost too easy, Mom."

"Not for me it isn't," Juliana corrected grimly. "I only ask that you wait until after you get back from Europe this summer before making your final decision."

Paige relaxed with an audible sigh. "That's reasonable. But this isn't just another crazy idea so don't get your hopes up."

"I won't. I promise, I won't." Juliana's heart swelled with love as she looked at her beautiful daughter. Impulsively she added, "I love you, sugar. I only want you to be happy."

"Now there's a switch." Paige paused at the doorway. "Not the part about loving me—I love you, too. But the 'happy' part . . . always before, you've said you only want what's best for me. Do I sense a subtle change here?"

"We can but hope." Juliana spoke flippantly, but she couldn't help thinking about it after Paige had gone to get ready for her date.

Happiness or what's best. Chocolate cake or liver. Ben or the whole wide world.

No contest.

THEY STOOD on the balcony, breathing the sweet night air. Clutching the sheet more tightly around her, Juliana turned her head to look at Ben, outlined by the lights from inside the house. He wore only an old pair of denim cutoffs that exposed his heavily muscled thighs and sleekly tapering knees and calves. When he turned toward her, the washboard rippling of his torso stood out boldly.

But she mustn't think of that now. Desperately she tried to work up the courage to tell him about Barbara, about Charlie and Mrs. Holmes. Unfortunately, when that was done Juliana would also have to tell Ben about herself.

She could swear on a stack of Bibles that she didn't remember a thing about the transaction in question, but that didn't excuse her. As the broker, she was legally and morally responsible.

Furthermore, she felt duty bound to admit to Ben that she'd bent the rules in the past—nothing illegal and nothing *too* immoral. Or at least, she didn't think so. After much soul searching, she still wasn't entirely sure. Her confidence had been too severely shaken.

Ben came up behind her and kissed her shoulder. "You're tense," he murmured, sliding his arms around her waist.

"Am I?" She flexed her shoulder blades against him. She'd arrived more than an hour ago and he'd enticed her directly into the bedroom—admittedly, without complaint or resistance on her part. Their lovemaking had been wonderful, even racked with guilt as she was.

"I think you missed me." He nuzzled the curve of her shoulder and she felt the damp flick of his tongue. His hands covered her breasts and squeezed gently. "Move in with me, Juli."

She groaned and closed her eyes. "Then neither of us would ever get anything done. The a-avocados would shrivel up—"

"To hell with avocados."

"And the Burtons would never find anyone to figure out what their problem is, let alone solve it."

He put his hands on her bare shoulders and turned her toward him. "I'm serious," he said in his husky voice.

"I know you are," she said miserably. She drew a shaky breath. "After I say what I'm about to say, you may change your mind."

SHE SAT at the kitchen table, the sheet draped around her. Filled with melancholy, she watched him make a pot of tea, his movements relaxed and easy. Even in her current state of depression she found herself admiring the sleek brown skin of his torso and the muscled strength of his legs.

He placed two mugs on the table, the strings and tags of the tea bags flopping. He sat down across from her and gave her a quizzical look.

So she told him. About Charlie Gresham and the widow Holmes, about Barbara's accusations and Stella's corroboration. She told it all, without once looking at him.

When she had finished, he spoke without inflection. "So Barbara all but called you a crook and you took it."

She didn't know how to defend herself. "Can you blame me? There are great gaps in my memory. Even when I do remember something, I don't trust it so I'm constantly trying to check."

"This is one you don't have to check."

Her head jerked up. "Why not?"

"Because I already did. I talked to Stella."

Juliana groaned. "Then you know I was all set to help Charlie Gresham cheat a poor widow."

"I know nothing of the kind." His face hardened to bronze. In the fluorescent lighting, his hair gleamed with shades of silver and gold.

"But you said—" Helplessly she spread her hands palms up.

Ben let out his breath in an explosive sigh, the muscles of his chest bunching as he leaned forward in his chair. "You're mighty damned eager to believe the worst. You don't have a very high opinion of yourself, do you."

"Why, I—" How could she? It sounded like an open and shut case. "Stella herself said I knew about the deal."

"Yes, but she never said you *understood* it. When I spoke to her after you left today, she realized that she'd been asking you to make decisions and offer guidance long before you were able to handle it. She's as upset about all this as you are—only she's mad as hell at herself, not at you."

Juliana reached for her cup, her hands trembling so badly that tea slopped over the rim. She snatched her hands back and dried them on the sheet. "I honestly don't remember anything about Mrs. Holmes or her property."

"I believe you," he said.

"How can you, when I'm not sure I believe myself?" She twisted the corners of the sheet into a knot. "I know I've never been a Pollyanna in business—"

"Or anything else," he inserted.

She glared at him. "This is serious, damn it. I know my reputation. I like—*liked* to think of myself as tough but honest. Now all of a sudden I have to wonder... Is this the kind of thing I did all the time? Maybe I can't remember because I don't want to remember. How can I be sure? How can you be sure?"

He leaned forward, propping an elbow on the table and resting his chin on his hand. "I'm sure," he said flatly.

She banged both fists down on the table, hard. The cup jumped and tea sprayed out, but she didn't even look at it. "But how can you believe in me?"

He didn't react to her anger and frustration. Instead he smiled. "Because I want to," he said simply. "That's what it always comes down to, in the end. The evidence against you is purely circumstantial—the jury could go either way. So I believe in you because I choose to."

Time stood still as she stared into his eyes, looking for the bait, the hook. She didn't realize she was crying until she could no longer see him through the tears.

He leaned across the table and picked up her hand. Her fingers tightened convulsively around his, and he let her cry.

Finally she swallowed hard and dabbed at her eyes with one corner of the sheet. "Thanks," she said, her voice husky. "I'm not used to having someone else believe in me more strongly than I do myself."

"Not a bad feeling, though."

"A wonderful feeling." She drew a shuddering breath. "I'm glad that's out in the open. I feel like I'm copping a plea, though. Between Charlie and Barbara—"

"Forget them. Juli, you've got to consider motives. Barbara hates your guts and always has, according to Stella. Even if Barbara believes everything she says, she's putting her own spin on it. Why shouldn't you do the same?" He gave her a mock-ferocious glare and tightened his hold on her hand. "As for Charlie, Stella said you took him in over your own best judgment because he was desperate. You were trying to do a good deed, Juli. Stella says you did a lot of nice things for people, you just weren't comfortable about letting anyone—"

He stiffened and looked toward the door with a frown.

"What is it?" she asked, instantly alarmed.

He cocked his head for a few seconds and listened, then shrugged. "Nothing, I guess. Sounded like a car engine there for a minute. But nobody comes up here, especially at this time of night. Where was I?"

"Something about Stella."

"Oh, yeah. You know how they say no man's a hero to his valet? I think it's equally true that no woman's a hero—make that heroine—to her secretary. Nobody knows you better professionally than Stella, and she's your biggest booster."

Again he hesitated. This time he listened for a second or two and then surged to his feet, fists clenching at his sides as he faced the door.

Juliana's heart plunged and she shrank back in her chair, clutching the sheet more tightly around her breasts. She wasn't afraid in a physical sense; she had absolute confidence in Ben's ability to protect her.

But she was very much afraid in every other sense. The thought of being discovered half-naked in the middle of the night in a man's kitchen practically sent her into a swoon.

Someone was definitely out there. The doorknob turned and the door began to swing open. Ben stepped forward, wrapped his fingers around the edge of the door and slammed it wide with such force that it banged against the wall and bounced back again to hit him in the shoulder, a blow he shrugged off.

"Oh!" A middle-aged woman stood on the step, one hand at her throat, her lips parted in astonishment. For a moment she stared into Ben's face, and then her glance slipped past him to settle on Juliana.

Ben grabbed the woman in a bear hug, completely screening her from Juliana's horrified gaze. "Damn it, Lil," he said explosively. "You might at least have let me know you were coming."

10

JULIANA SPRANG to her feet, tugging the sheet up beneath her arms. She had to get out of here. Moving stealthily, she turned toward the doorway. With her second step her foot came down on the dragging tail of fabric, all but ripping the sheet from her hands.

"Looks as if I've come at a bad time."

Lillian's amused tone made Juliana's entire scalp prickle and she stood with bowed head, caught. Doomed. She heard their voices; they were having fun at her expense, all right.

"If I'm not mistaken, that's Juliana Malone I see trying to skulk out of here."

"Naw. Juliana wouldn't *skulk*. She'd *run*."

Sheepishly, Juliana turned, hoisting the sheet up with both hands. She took a deep breath, straightened her shoulders and dredged up her most sparkling smile. "Lillian! What a surprise."

Lillian burst into great peals of laughter. She was a large-boned woman, broad shouldered and substantial, like her brother. Gray streaked her blond hair, and her face radiated good humor.

"Hi, hon." She crossed the room and gave Juliana a hug that knocked the sheet askew once more. "Fancy meeting you here."

Juliana gave a self-conscious little laugh. "That goes double for me." Her flustered glance took in brother and sister. "If you two will excuse me, I'll just go slip into something a little more ... more."

"Does that mean you won't be spending the night?"

Ben's blunt question stopped her in her tracks. She groaned and gave him an offended glance over one shoulder. Beside him, Lillian raised her eyebrows in spurious innocence.

Cheeks burning, Juliana sailed from the room. She returned ten minutes later, blue silk shirt neatly tucked into tailored white slacks. At her entrance, Ben and Lillian glanced up from their conversation at the table.

"Look," Juliana began uncomfortably, "I'll just go on home and let the two of you talk."

Lillian smiled. "Don't be silly. Sit down here with us." She patted a chair. "I'm sorry I teased you, but you looked so ... teasable. This may shock you, but people in Santa Barbara fool around once in a while, too, so I do know about such things."

Juliana slipped into the indicated chair. "I'm new at this," she confessed. "I guess I'm just too old-fashioned to take discovery in stride."

Lillian patted Juliana's shoulder. "Ben's new at it, too," she confided in a richly indulgent voice. "Nothing on earth could have made me happier than *not* finding my brother alone."

"Nothing except a speedy exit from the avocado business and a big fat check." Ben sounded bitter.

Lillian's good humor slipped away. "I said I'd go along with you as long as I can," she said bluntly. "But the bills on this place were piling up even before Mother died, and there hasn't been a nickel of profit since."

"I sold $36,000 worth of avocados last month," Ben shot back.

"Yes, and used it against $75,000 in bills," Lillian retorted.

"Mind if we talk about this later?"

Lillian's lips tightened. "It won't change anything. I don't want to fight you on this, but I can't afford an expensive hobby and neither can you." She stood up. "Look, my eyes are killing me. I've got to get these contacts out before I go blind. I'll be right back."

Juliana and Ben sat quietly until Lillian had gone off toward the bathroom. Then Juliana sighed. "I'm sorry." She reached across the table and touched his hand. "Anything I can do to help?"

He gave her a narrow-eyed glance. "You're not offering to find a buyer, are you?"

"No!" She slapped his hand lightly. She hesitated; she had the perfect solution, if he'd just be reasonable. "I'm offering you a loan," she said tentatively.

He stiffened and his blue eyes darkened. "No chance." He snarled the words. "There are names for men who accept money from women."

"Yes—husbands!" It just popped out. She stared at him, aghast. "I'm sorry. I didn't mean that."

His tense face relaxed a little. "The hell you didn't." He lifted her hand to his mouth. "You suggesting I marry you for your money?"

"Certainly not." She strove for indignation, but settled for breathless anticipation as he lifted her arm until his lips could press against the pulse throbbing in her wrist.

His eyes teased her. "But you did mention the word *husband*."

"I was just being funny." His lips slipped down to the inner curve of her elbow and she choked on the last word.

"Funny ha-ha or funny strange?" He kissed his way up her arm to her shoulder.

"Funny wonderful." She shivered as he leaned toward her. He blew in her ear and she groaned with pleasure, then darted an anxious glance toward the door through which his sister had disappeared. "Could we talk about this later?" She closed her eyes and sighed.

"Nope." He nibbled on her ear. "If you ever mention the word 'loan' to me again it'll be the end of a beautiful relationship."

"That's right." Lillian's voice intruded. She stood in the doorway, grinning. "He can be had, but he can't be bought."

Juliana hauled back against Ben's grip, but he hung on. He gave his sister a crooked grin. "I sure am glad you dropped by, Lil. When you leaving?"

Lillian made a face at him. "Tomorrow or the next day. Will you kindly fetch in my overnight case from the car?" She added to Juliana, "My husband's all tied up with inventory at his hardware store so I decided to come down on the spur of the moment."

Juliana watched Ben throw the door wide and walk outside. In the few seconds it was open, Freeloader streaked between his ankles and into the room. Ben didn't seem to notice as he let the screen slam closed. But Lillian did.

"What an adorable kitten!" She leaned over and rubbed her thumb and fingers together lightly, trying to entice the animal to her. "Kitty-kitty-kitty."

Freeloader arched his back coyly, gave her a haughty glance and hot-footed it through the room and down the hall.

Lillian straightened, her expression puzzled. "I don't believe it."

"What?"

"That Ben's got a cat." Lillian turned eyes almost as blue as her brother's on Juliana. "Something that depends on him. . . . Ben used to thrive on responsibility, but not since his wife and son died."

"He . . . he doesn't say much about that."

"He wouldn't. He felt responsible, although of course he wasn't. He thought he'd failed in his duty to his family, his job, even to society. He didn't figure he was worth the powder and lead it'd take to blow him to hell—his words, not mine."

Juliana's heart constricted. "I wish I'd been there," she whispered, realizing even as she said it that there could have been nothing between them then, especially not understanding.

"No you don't." Lillian looked grim. "He went down the tubes—for two years he did everything short of drugs. He'd been a cop too long—he couldn't do drugs even to punish himself. But he—" She shook her head and drew a quivering breath. "I shouldn't be talking like this. I guess it's just that. . .at the moment, I feel more optimistic about my brother than I have in a long time."

Juliana lifted her brows in question. "Because he has a cat?"

Lillian nodded. "And a woman."

The screen door slammed and Juliana started. Ben entered, carrying a flight bag and a couple of plastic grocery sacks. "You imported food from Santa Barbara? Hey, we got supermarkets down here and everything."

"Last time I was here, you were eating avocados for breakfast, lunch and dinner. I wasn't taking any chances." Lillian rose and took the plastic bags from him.

Juliana also stood up. "I've really got to be going," she said. "I hope I see you again before you leave, Lillian."

"Me, too."

Ben dropped Lillian's bag on the floor and reached for Juliana's hand. "C'm'on, I'll walk you to the car."

He held the door, then winked jauntily at his sister before following Juliana out.

BEN AND LILLIAN sat up late that night, drinking cup after cup of coffee and talking. They had always been close, despite the ten-year age difference—perhaps because of it, Ben sometimes thought. In some ways Lillian was more mother than sister, but she was also a trusted friend.

Tonight, though, she was a business partner, and as such deserved the unvarnished truth. So Ben gave it to her.

"You remember that stretch of hot weather we had in April? Four hundred-degree days in a row.... Fruit dropped like hailstones. Opal says I lost about thirty percent of my crop, but that's not even the worst of it. The new buds were coming in and it hurt them, too."

Lillian gave an exasperated snort. "And you still think you can make a go of this place?"

"Yes, *if* I have a decent crop in August. And that'll happen, *if* we don't get any real bad Santa Anas, and *if* I can hold the irrigation system together and *if*—"

"I get the picture." She got up and refilled her cup from the pot on the stove. "I'd think you'd want to sell and get out from under all that."

He was shaking his head before she finished speaking. "I don't, and especially not to that bastard."

"Your lady friend works for that 'bastard,' as you call him."

"Don't remind me. The guy dangles big commissions in front of her and she salivates like one of Pavlov's dogs. Or did. She says she's changed."

"And you believe her?" Lillian's brows arched.

He sat there for a minute, thinking about that. Finally he said simply, "Yes." He sighed. "Life'd sure be simpler if I could just sell off a few acres, but Goddard's got the valley so tied up that there's no chance of that."

"You or him, huh, with Juliana in the middle. Not a very comfortable place to be."

Ben frowned. "I never thought of it that way."

Lillian nodded. "Knowing she was handling the sale before Mom died, you could have knocked me over with a feather when I walked in here and found the two of you together in a delightfully compromising situation."

Remembering Juliana's discomfiture, Ben laughed. "You could have knocked her over with a feather, too. She's still having a hard time adjusting."

Lillian gave him an assessing glance. "I'm about to overstep the bounds of good sisterhood," she announced. "Ben, do you really care for her or is this just a...a fling?"

The question didn't surprise him in the slightest; what surprised him was the ease with which he could answer it. "Flings aren't my thing, Lil."

"Then we're talking Serious Relationship?"

"Maybe."

"That's an awfully big step for you." She looked at him, love shining in her eyes. "I've prayed for this day. Are you hesitating because of Melanie?"

He waited for the familiar shaft of pain that the mention of his dead wife always brought. It did not come. Instead, he felt sadness, and a simple, healing regret for what could not be changed. "I'm not hesitating," he said. "I've asked Juliana to move in here with me, but she hasn't made up her mind." He shifted restlessly. "It's late. You about ready to hit the hay?"

Her steady gaze made him want to squirm. "Something else is bothering you. What is it?"

He felt cold all over, and he shivered before he could catch himself. "Nothing," he said. "Plenty. I'm not sure I'm being fair to her. She had brain surgery a few months ago, for Christ's sake. You don't get over something like that overnight. She thinks she's feeling love, but what if it's gratitude, or simply insecurity?"

He lunged to his feet, fists clenching at his sides. "I'm going to bed," he said. He left her sitting there alone.

JULIANA CLUTCHED the telephone receiver until her knuckles whitened, forcing herself to remain calm. "But Cary, it doesn't make sense," she argued. "I know we have a contract, but I'll tell you flat out that Ben won't sell to you and I'm through trying to get him to change his mind."

"Ah, so you have been trying."

"I meant *before*. I tried to get him to change his mind before, but not anymore. I can't work for you any longer, Cary. I'll return all fees and commissions, but I won't honor the buyer-broker agreement."

"I'll pay double."

She groaned. "Money isn't the issue."

"Money is always the issue. Use your head—you don't want to throw away all those bucks."

A lot of bucks, a lot of bucks, a lot of bucks—money is always the issue. A horrible feeling of déjà vu washed over her and she gasped; for an instant she was back in the hospital, the wrathful voices of Ben and Cary dueling in her brain. The receiver fell from her numb fingers and clattered against the desk. It took a moment of fumbling before she got back on line.

"I dropped the phone," she choked out, painfully aware of the quaver in her voice. "I'm sorry, but I can't work for you anymore. If I have to I'll simply sit here until our contract expires in October, but there's nothing I can do for you."

"Damn it, you can't get away with this."

"I'm sorry. Goodbye, Cary."

She hung up, her entire body trembling. She stared down at her hands, seeing the short nails, but remembering when they had been otherwise.

It had been a long time since she'd experienced such a strong flash of recall. She'd learned to live with an occasional problem of expression—a word or phrase that refused to come—and a fluctuating ability to recall numbers and names and events. But for an instant there, she'd gone all the way back, back to a nightmarish struggle for survival itself.

LILLIAN WENT HOME a couple of days later and Juliana was sorry—but not very. She liked Ben's sister, but she liked Ben more, and Lillian's presence cut seriously into their time together.

Also, business was booming, and gradually she settled back into that groove. But now she watched every move she made, not trusting herself. For the first time she felt drawn not to the big bucks but to the challenges. She spent all the time she could with Ben, but somehow it was never enough.

Paige left for Europe on the sixteenth day of June in the company of a dozen other students, the group led by an art instructor from the local community college. That same afternoon, Juliana moved in with Ben.

"I don't know why you waited," he groused as he carried an armload of her clothing, still on hangers, into the house. "Who'd you think you're fooling? Certainly not Paige."

"I'm just not ready to get into this with her or anybody else." Juliana looked around for a likely place to deposit the cardboard box of underwear she clutched in her arms.

He dumped his burden onto the bed. "You ashamed of what you're doing, Juli?"

He looked so big and strong and sexy standing there beside the bed that she felt her pulse accelerate. "I'm not ashamed," she said, her voice low. "But neither am I interested in spreading my personal business all over town."

She set the box on top of the dresser and hesitated, watching him in the mirror. "I've never done anything like this before—lived with a man I wasn't married to, I mean. Let me get used to it before I go public, okay?"

"I suppose." His level blue gaze seemed to strip her bare. "Think cohabitation will be bad for business?"

"If I did, I wouldn't be here." She spoke tartly but not honestly, despite her almost daily pledges to herself to tell nothing but the truth. She groaned. "I don't mean that. The truth is, I'm not sure *what* it will mean where business is concerned. But I've decided you're worth the risk."

He stared at her, then threw back his head and laughed, the cords in his thick brown neck standing out. He held out his arms to her.

"Avocados be damned," he said.

"Ditto real estate." She met him more than halfway.

His words began to seem almost prophetic, in light of the continuing drought. The avocado business really *did* seem to be damned as July approached with ever-rising temperatures and ever-lower humidity.

Although attracting more and more attention and business as a security consultant, Ben spent every available minute in the groves, struggling to keep the aging irrigation system operational and the trees watered and cared for.

He'd been close-mouthed about the farm's prospects since Lillian's visit, and so Juliana wasn't prepared for his terse appraisal one evening over the dinner table.

"If this weather doesn't break, I'm going to start losing the good stuff."

His comment seemed to come at Juliana out of left field. She'd been talking about the real estate ball, and it took her a few seconds to switch gears. "The good stuff?"

"The heavy fruit drops first, before it's ready to pick." He stared down at the avocado on his plate as if it were at fault. He shoved his fork at the shrimp stuffing without enthusiasm.

Juliana—who'd gone to a lot of trouble to stop by the supermarket and pick up the shrimp, not to mention the time she'd spent peeling it—watched with displeasure. "Can't you just pick the avocados up off the ground and sell them?"

"Sure, but they're bruised and not worth a hell of a lot." He banged his fork down. "It's not working," he said. "If it wasn't for the money I bring in with the security consulting, it'd be over already."

"Oh, Ben, why won't you let me help?"

It was an ongoing point of contention between them, although rarely acknowledged openly. He shook his head. "No chance." He sat in silence for a moment and then said abruptly, "I got a new offer on the place today. It's lower than what Goddard was willing to pay, but I may decide to take it."

Juliana caught her breath sharply. *No! This deal is mine!* The thought flashed across her mind closely followed by the realization that such a reaction was completely unworthy of her. "W-who's the agent?"

"Barbara Snell."

Another blow. She swallowed hard and tried to keep her voice calm and noncommittal. "Who's the buyer?"

"Some company from L.A. I never heard of it, but the plans aren't a lot different from Goddard's."

"But you're considering it?" She pushed her plate away, her own appetite gone.

"Yeah. The hell of it is, I know I could make this farm work if I just had a little more time." The muscle in his jaw ridged. "Looks like probate will be settled within the next six weeks. There are bills, and Lillian's got to see some bucks."

But he won't accept a loan from me, Juliana reminded herself. "Is...is there anything at all I can do to help you?"

He turned a serious face toward her. "Yeah. If I sell, I want you to handle it for me."

She still had a buyer-broker agreement with Cary Goddard; she wondered what her legal position was if she helped Ben sell to someone else. She swallowed hard. "Sure."

"At your usual commission."

"Forget it!" She jumped to her feet and began clearing the table, trying to work off her outrage. Here she was, doing her damnedest to reform, and he offered her *money*?

They'd reached an impasse and they both knew it. By mutual consent they dropped the subject for the time being.

JULIANA SAT IN A BOOTH at The Hungry Munchkin, patiently waiting for Rodney Burton to pause for breath so she could ease the conversation back in the appropriate direction. Helen Burton sat beside him, her sweet face wearing a pained expression.

Juliana had spent untold hours with the Burtons, her initial reluctance rapidly changing into a determination to boldly go where no real-estate professional had ever been—to a solution for the Burtons' real-estate problems.

Rodney's booming tones drew the attention of nearby diners. "Well, I won't stand for it," he announced. "I won't be taken advantage of by some pipsqueak who has no respect for his elders." He frowned, his bushy white brows drawing together as he fixed his eagle eye on Juliana. "You, on the other hand, seem more in tune with the high standards and principles of my generation. Therefore I've decided to give you carte blanche to handle my real-estate business, young woman. You may proceed."

Rodney leaned back against the upholstered backrest and gave her a look that placed complete responsibility for the outcome of their association on her shoulders. Helen breathed a gentle sigh of relief.

Juliana figured that by the time this association ended, she'd probably be earning an hourly wage slightly less than that accorded baby-sitters, but what the hell? She'd do it for the challenge.

And because it gave her a plausible reason to avoid a return to the real-estate fast track.

By the time the Burtons departed forty minutes later, she felt limp as a dishrag. No wonder dealing with Rodney Burton made strong men weep, she thought as she watched them walk out of the restaurant. Rodney, as usual, kept up a running commentary, and Helen gazed up at him with adoration on her lined face.

That woman must be a saint, Juliana thought, not for the first time. Or...new idea...there must be a great deal more to Rodney than was apparent to the casual observer. At any rate, she was convinced that the worst hurdle was behind them—Rodney trusted her.

She started to rise and her glance met that of a woman across the room. *Barbara Snell—just what I need*, she thought. The two women hadn't spoken since the confrontation in Juliana's office. Now she nodded to Barbara, then glanced at her companion—and did a double take.

Cary Goddard sat across from Barbara, a smile on his handsome face. Juliana dropped back into her chair, all the breath knocked out of her. She hadn't even known Cary was in town. *What the hell's going on?*

As she watched, Cary rose, said something to Barbara and turned directly toward Juliana's booth. His glance met hers. For a moment he hesitated, and then he started forward.

Juliana's heart pounded. She'd mailed him a check and a letter stating her intent to cancel their business relationship, but no way could he have received it already. Oh, if only she hadn't procrastinated! Now he was going to lean on her about Ben's land and she'd immediately be on the defensive.

He stopped beside the booth. "Mind if I join you?" He sat down.

The question being now moot, Juliana shrugged. "I'm surprised to see you here. I didn't know you were in town."

"I didn't think you'd care."

She recoiled slightly at his tone, which seemed vaguely reproachful. "Why do you say that?" she faltered.

He shrugged with exaggerated innocence. "Now that you're living with Ben Ware...."

She would not let him see a reaction, but she couldn't hide her response from herself. Her stomach clenched and her throat closed with mortification. "Who told you that?" she demanded.

"Doesn't matter." He picked up a fork and traced invisible patterns on the white linen tablecloth. "Under the circumstances, I've decided to let you off the hook. If you'd leveled with me the first time we spoke, told me you were personally involved with Ware. . . ." His narrowed glance slammed into her. "But you didn't." He stood up. "Enough said. Consider our professional association at an end."

She took her courage in hand. "And our personal association? Cary, I hope we can part without hard feelings. Perhaps someday—"

"Someday?" His carefully controlled expression slipped and for an instant the merciless tycoon stood there. "I don't take any man's leavings, Juliana. I can only assume you're suggesting there is a remote possibility we can do business together again someday."

"I was hoping we could avoid hard feel—"

He cut her off ruthlessly. "Bring me Benjamin Ware's head on a platter and we'll talk."

She sat in stunned silence while he threaded his way through the restaurant toward the men's room. Somehow when he spoke of Ben's head on a platter, it didn't sound like rhetoric.

She was still trying to steady herself when Barbara approached.

"Oh, good," Juliana said, too distracted to play her usual game of "what good friends we are" with the woman. "You here to finish me off?"

"I don't know what you're talking about," Barbara said airily. Without asking, she slipped into the seat recently vacated by Cary. "I just wanted to commend you, about Edna Holmes. It took some pressure, but at least you finally did the right thing."

Juliana started to explain, started to tell Barbara that it was all a mistake, but stopped before uttering a word.

What was the point? Barbara would believe exactly what she chose to believe.

As Ben believed what he chose to believe. Juliana relaxed slightly. "You old flatterer you. You'll turn my head."

"No, really, I can see you're a changed woman. Finding you here with the Burtons proves that." Barbara's little-girl voice reeked with sincerity. "Gosh, Juliana, if you manage to solve their problem, you'll be doing a big favor to the entire real-estate community."

Barbara's expression said very plainly that such an occurrence was not even within the realm of possibility. Well, Juliana thought, she who laughs last... "I'm here to serve," she said dryly.

"Aren't we all. Pull it off with Rodney Burton and your name will go down in history." Barbara poked a finger at salt grains on the tablecloth. "Will Ben Ware be escorting you to the real estate ball next month?"

So you're the blabbermouth, Juliana thought. She kept her voice noncommittal. "I suppose so." At one time, the ball had been the highlight of her year, since her office was always amply represented by award winners. But since leaving the hospital, she'd hardly given the event a thought. In all honesty, she admitted to herself, that might be because she no longer stood even an outside chance of snagging the Real Estate Star prize.

Barbara cleared her throat. "I wonder if he's said anything to you about the offer I brought in on his property."

Ah, now we get down to it, Juliana thought. "He mentioned it."

"I thought he might ask you to represent him." Barbara's baby-blue eyes narrowed shrewdly. "It's a good offer."

"Not as good as the one from Goddard Enterprises."

"But you and I both know Ben won't sell to Goddard Enterprises, at least, not—" Barbara broke off abruptly.

Juliana supplied the rest of the sentence which seemed to hang out there somewhere, unspoken. "Not . . . *knowingly*." She stared at the other woman. "The offer *is* from Cary, isn't it?"

"I said no such thing." Barbara sounded a bit flustered. She stood up. "Just because I'm having lunch with the man doesn't mean anything."

"Some L.A. company made the offer, Ben said. Cary's corporate headquarters is in L.A."

"So are a jillion others. Juliana, if you're interested in Ben's welfare at all, advise him to sell. He's sitting on a gold mine out there, but he's just about pushed the gentleman-farmer act as far as it will go. This is the best offer he's going to get. The ante is already dropping."

Past Barbara's shoulder, Juliana saw Cary reenter the room, look at his now vacant table for Barbara and then glance around. He saw her with Juliana and his step faltered—just one step, but Juliana saw, and she knew.

And knowing, she felt sick to her stomach. Everything Barbara had said about Ben's situation was true, but it appeared he'd rather lose everything than sell to Cary Goddard.

Cary was behind this second offer just as sure as avocados are green. She had to tell Ben, she told herself. Just as soon as she got the chance.

BEN ALREADY had too much on his mind, so she kept putting off telling him about Cary, and then it was too late. "Honey," he said a couple of days later, "I've been thinking about that offer Barbara brought me. If push comes to shove, I'm gonna take it."

Juliana, elbow-deep in sudsy dishwater, stiffened. *Why, oh, why didn't I blow the whistle on Cary when I had the chance?* she thought, berating herself. Now she'd lost the initiative. "About that offer . . ." she began carefully.

He picked up a dish towel and reached for a plate in the dish drainer. "There's still half a chance it won't come to that." He dried the plate and stacked it inside the open cabinet. "But if it does, that's my decision."

He wrapped his arms around her waist, managing to dip the tail of his dish towel in the wash pan in the process. He pulled her back against him, leaning down to nuzzle her ear.

"It's less money than Goddard Enterprises offered," she reminded him cautiously.

"I know. But it's worth it to me. I'll make up the difference to Lillian from my share . . . if it comes to that. But I still believe in miracles."

"Right," she agreed, but she was lying. She simply couldn't see any miracles on the horizon.

Much later, long after Ben had drifted off to sleep, she lay beside him in the four-poster bed and wrestled with her options—and her conscience.

She could tell him Cary was behind the offer from Barbara and that would be the end of that. But then what would he do if the avocado crop failed?

Or she could keep quiet—even encourage the sale—and hope that when Ben found out the identity of the real buyer, as he surely would, he'd never realize Juliana knew and hadn't warned him.

Bad choices, both of them. But for the longest time, she couldn't think of any third possibility.

Then when she did, it scared her so much she spent a sleepless night trying to talk herself out of it.

11

JULIANA WAS WAITING at Señor Pizza when Pete arrived to open up the next morning.

He gave her a startled look. "What's wrong?"

"Nothing. Let's go inside so we can talk."

He unlocked the front door and led her through the restaurant to his office. "I don't think I'm going to like this, but let's have it," he said darkly.

She drew a shaky breath. "Pete, I need a favor."

"I figured that much out already."

"I—" she licked dry lips "—I want you to buy a few acres of Ben's land. I'll handle the arrangements and put up the money. All I need from you is a signature. We'll have a trust company handle it and no one will know we're even involved."

Pete let out his breath in an explosive gust of sound. "What the hell are you up to?"

"I'm not up to anything." She gritted her teeth. She was so *damned* tired of always justifying herself. "Ben's desperate for money. He won't take a penny from me and he won't sell to Goddard Enterprises."

"There goes your commission right out of the window."

"Save the cracks for someone who'll appreciate your wit." His attitude set her teeth on edge, but she tried to control herself because she needed him. "In order to keep my name entirely out of it, I've got to have a front man and you're it."

"I thought you were working for Cary Goddard." His lip curled. "This whole thing sounds fishy to me."

She straightened her shoulders. "If it'll make you feel any better, I'll give you my word. I'm trying to help Ben, not hurt him."

"Like you used to help me. You always know what's best for other people."

That hurt. She fixed him with an unfriendly stare. "You really have a low opinion of me."

He didn't bat an eye. "Experience is the best teacher. I can just see you a few months down the road, after your infatuation for Ben or whatever it is has passed. You'll have some very valuable property to ease your grief."

She gritted her teeth and glared at him. Ben believed in her; why couldn't Pete? "Look," she said brusquely, "I could stand here and talk until I'm blue in the face and I still won't convince you unless you want to be convinced. So I'll put it to you flat—I want you to do this on faith."

For a long time he stood there, his face tense as he considered. She waited, calm on the outside and a mass of nerves inside.

Finally he nodded. "Okay," he said sharply, unhappily.

The starch went out of her and her shoulders slumped. "You won't be sorry."

"I'm already sorry, but I'm not surprised. Not really." A new note had entered his voice, a bitter note of disappointment.

"What's that supposed to mean?"

He turned accusing eyes on her. "That nobody gets a ten-thousand-dollar windfall without strings attached. When you gave me that check you said you'd think of some way for me to repay you. You weren't kidding, were you?"

She started to defend herself, but stopped short. He wouldn't believe her anyway.

IN MID-JULY, ten days before the realtors' ball, the Santa Ana struck with a vengeance, bearing dry desert winds through Buena Suerte Valley and on to the coast. Temperatures soared into the nineties and vegetation began to shrivel and die.

Watching, Juliana prayed for that miracle. But just in case none was forthcoming, everything was in place: the instant Pete gave the word, Ben would receive a new offer on two-and-one-half acres fronting on Buena Suerte Canyon Road. And Pete would give the word at Juliana's command.

She hoped—prayed—it was a command that would never be given. Unless Ben's avocado operation went under, there'd be no need to activate her plan to help him whether he wanted help or not.

In the avocado groves, Ben worked like a madman, fighting the irrigation system. With continual high temperatures in the ground, a fungus began to build up in the water pipes like cholesterol in arteries. Eventually it clogged the water emitters, the three-inch-high sprinkler heads that actually delivered the water.

Ten emitters ringed each individual tree. With more than two thousand trees, Ben had his work cut out for him. A plunging device on each clogged sprinkler head had to be manipulated by hand; if that didn't do the trick, the easiest and quickest solution was replacement. But at almost a half dollar each, Ben simply didn't have the thousands of dollars that replacement would cost.

So he laboriously removed each clogged emitter and cleaned it in a bleach solution before replacing it. And all the time his water bill rose. Opal predicted it could soar to as much as $1,600 for the month of July alone.

On the fifth day of the Santa Ana, Ben got a third offer.

"This is incredible," he told Juliana excitedly over dinner that night. "I didn't think there was a prayer anyone would be willing to buy just a few acres, not with Goddard already owning half the valley and most of the access. If I sell off just these few acres, there's still a chance to keep the avocado operation nearly intact."

Juliana dropped her gaze to her salad bowl and poked at a ripe slice of avocado. "Then you're going to do it?"

Ben nodded. "It's sure as hell preferable to selling the whole enchilada. I told them I've got to have some time to think it over but—"

A pounding at the open kitchen door interrupted. Opal stood outside. When she had their attention, she walked in.

Juliana rose, smiling. Watching her, Ben realized she was quite comfortable now about having Opal around. Juliana didn't even seem aware that she wasn't wearing her wig. Her hair was growing out—short brown tendrils curved around her face, lending an appealing softness.

Opal knew, of course, that Juliana was living here now. He wondered when she'd be ready to let the rest of the world in on the secret.

"Have a seat, Opal, and I'll get you a glass of tea," Juliana invited.

"Thanks." The white-haired woman pulled out a chair and sat down, crossing her booted feet. "That's what I come by for, to say thanks."

Juliana set down a glass of ice and reached for the tea pitcher. "You're welcome."

Opal laughed. "Naw, not for the tea. For helping Rodney and Helen."

"Oh, that." Juliana resumed her seat. She was embarrassed. "They're nice people. It was no big deal."

"No big deal!" Opal hooted. "They're *my* friends and even *I* admit Rodney is not the easiest ol' boy to deal with."

Ben looked from one to the other. Juliana's success with the Burtons was news to him. "So what did you do?" he asked.

"Nothing fancy. The biggest problem was communication. Once I figured out their situation, it was fairly simple. I got them a reverse mortgage."

Ben's brows arched. "Is that what it sounds like? If it is, I'll take one."

Opal laughed. "It's only for old fogies," she said.

Juliana nodded. "Basically, that's right. A reverse mortgage converts the equity in a house into a monthly income with a deferred repayment schedule. That means they can go on living in their own home with money coming in each month. Repayment will come at some point down the road when the house is sold."

"By which time, they'll be six feet under and won't give a hoot."

Juliana rolled her eyes. "You do have a way with words, Opal."

"I sure do." Opal nodded. "So that's why I come to say thanks, Juliana. You're your father's daughter, all right, and no finer man ever lived. He'd be proud as a peacock of you, girl."

Juliana caught her breath, taken completely by surprise at such praise. "I . . . I was proud of him, too," she admitted.

And it was true. Finally and at long last, it was true. For perhaps the first time in her life, she felt nothing but pride in being compared with her father. So what if she hadn't made big bucks on the Burtons? It had been a real learning experience—she felt she ought to pay them! She laughed out loud at the thought.

THE HEAT WAVE stretched on interminably... six days, seven.... Grass and weeds turned brown and died on the hillsides, trees and bushes wilted in the fierce temperatures and low humidity. Wildlife—coyotes and snakes especially—began to appear in the groves more and more boldly in the search for water. But if the howl of coyotes didn't bother Ben, something else did.

"The worse sound an avocado grower can hear is plop...plop...plop," he said in a dispirited voice. "That's the sound of avocados falling off the trees."

Juliana went through her days holding her breath, waiting for Ben to make a final decision on the fate of the ranch. By now, she had cold feet and wasn't sure what she wanted him to do. It would make everything so much easier if he'd just swallow his pride long enough to accept a loan, she thought dejectedly.

Which of course, he wouldn't.

In the meantime, life went on. With Paige due to return from Europe the day after the real-estate ball, Juliana made reluctant plans to move back into her own house.

"When the going gets tough, the not-so-tough bail out," Ben said moodily. Juliana had spent most of the day trying to get her stuff organized for the move.

"That's not fair," she said tightly. "When I moved in here we both agreed—"

"I know what we agreed." He turned abruptly and headed for the door.

"Ben?"

He stopped, his back to her, his hand on the doorknob. His very posture seemed forbidding.

She forced herself to speak. "I have to drive to L.A. tomorrow. All my stuff will be moved by then, so I'll just go on home when I get back." *Beg me to stay—ask me to stay.* She held her breath.

Muscle ridged across his shoulders, beneath the soft white T-shirt. Then, ever so gradually, he relaxed.

"Suit yourself," he said carelessly. He opened the screen door.

"You'll still go to the ball with me, won't you?" Damn, it came out like a plea, as if she were begging. Well, maybe she was.

He shrugged. "Sure. Tickets cost money. I wouldn't want you to waste one." And he was gone.

That night in the four-poster bed, he roused her to a fever pitch she thought he'd never deign to satisfy. Even after he had—brilliantly—she found herself lying there in the dark and wondering if this was his way of telling her that although she could move back into her own house and resume her old life, nothing would ever be the same for her again.

As if she needed a reminder.

When she left for Los Angeles Friday, Ben didn't bother to come in from the grove to see her off. Not even Freeloader was around. She hoped the kitten was safely inside the barn; it had a dangerous tendency to wander around in the groves.

Dejected, she drove down from the rim of the canyon. Up on the terraced slopes, she caught a glimpse of Ben among the trees. She waved; he lifted one arm in a brief, dismissive gesture, a bronzed mythical figure.

The day passed in distracted attempts to concentrate on business. It wasn't until she turned the Mercedes toward Summerhill again that she admitted this wasn't going to work.

She didn't want to leave him. She didn't want to move back into her own house. The weeks she'd spent with him had been the happiest and most deeply satisfying of her life and she was about to turn her back on them and on him.

THE WIND BLEW IN from the deserts to the west, hot and dry and destructive as it picked up speed. Temperatures hovered in the upper nineties and the molten sun blazed from a cloudless sky.

Ben squatted in the deep leafy ground cover beneath an avocado tree, shaded by the thick canopy of branches. Digging down, he located the flexible black irrigation pipe and pulled it free of debris.

Carefully he examined the pipe. Several of the sprinkler heads were missing, and he saw tooth marks around the punctures in the pipe where they'd been. Coyotes. The wild things were suffering, too.

Hell of a business, he thought with disgust, throwing down the pipe and rising. He'd been in the groves since Juliana drove away. It was time to go back to the house and face up to the emptiness he would find there.

As he neared the barn, Freeloader trotted out into the road ahead and sat down to groom itself. Ben grinned at the creature. At least the cat was sticking.

Would Juliana have stuck if Ben sold this place? The thought was new and unwelcome and Ben stopped to consider it. A flash of movement brought his head swinging up just in time to see a gray shadow dart out of the shady depths of the grove and streak toward Freeloader straight as an arrow.

"Coyote!" Ben yelled and hurled himself forward into a run. At his warning cry, Freeloader sprang up, the hair of its back rising. *Stupid cat doesn't know where the dan-*

ger's coming from, Ben realized as the creature spun in a circle as if trying to figure out what the hell was going on.

Too late the cat saw the coyote. Without slowing its breakneck pace it swung its head and snatched Freeloader up in its jaws, never breaking stride.

Muscles straining, Ben charged after the marauder, dodging and ducking beneath the low, heavy branches of the avocado trees. Hopelessly outmatched, he watched the coyote pull away, its skinny, rangy form sliding effortlessly beneath low-hanging branches. The cat flopped bonelessly in the creature's mouth.

Ben's breath labored in his lungs as he fought his way between the trees. He knew he was too late; he knew the kitten was dead, and even if he caught up to the coyote there was nothing he could do. But he kept running.

The toes of one foot hooked beneath an irrigation pipe and he pitched forward full length on the soft cushion of leaves. Swearing, he scrambled up just in time to see the coyote disappear down an embankment leading to the road.

Heart pounding, Ben reached the point where the coyote had vanished, along with its helpless prey. Nothing. No sign of cat or captor.

Freeloader was history. Ben's head tilted back and a monstrous cry of denial ripped from his straining throat. *I've failed again.* The realization clawed at his gut. *Everything I touch turns to—*

He saw the Mercedes out of the corner of his eye, snaking along the canyon road below. Juliana was coming back, despite all her protestations to the contrary.

Without thinking, he flung himself over the lip of the embankment, his feet scrambling and slipping as he plummeted down the slope to intercept her.

BEN HURTLED into the road ahead and Juliana slammed on the brakes. Her heart pounded—he looked like a wild man—bits of leaves clinging to his tousled hair, his torn T-shirt stained with earth and sweat. His arms were scratched and beaded with bloody furrows and his face bore an expression barbaric in its ferocity.

She threw open the car door and jumped out, eager and yet somehow frightened.

Ben stalked toward her and she waited, trembling. His massive chest rose and fell with the force of his breathing, and she saw the beauty of an avenging angel in his face and body.

He grabbed her by the arms and hauled her body close but not quite touching. His blue eyes glared down into her face. "I love you," he said in his raspy voice. "Don't ever leave me again."

He yanked her hard against him, so tightly that she felt every bulge and indentation in his lean hard length. His hot mouth found hers; his tongue plunged between her lips almost brutally, as if he were branding her with the mark of his possession.

At last he raised his head. Cupping her face with his hands, he stared down at her. Somehow her wig had slipped off and he slid one hand over her scalp, his fingers sliding through the short brown hair.

"You came back," he said in a voice rough with emotion. "I need you, Juliana, and I love you. Marry me."

Her hands were at his waist beneath his T-shirt, and she clenched her fingers convulsively into his lean sides. Unendurable happiness welled up inside her, so intense that she scarcely dared believe in it. "W-what did you say?"

"You know perfectly well what I said." He gave her a hard, fast kiss on the lips. "Say yes, Juliana. Don't think about it, don't consider what impact it would have on your business, don't analyze it to death. Just say yes!"

"Yes!" She reached up to smooth his blond hair away from the side of his face in a loving gesture.

He drew a ragged breath. "You mean it?" His voice sounded dubious, as if he, too, were afraid to hope.

"I mean it. Ben, I love you." She rose on tiptoe and pressed fevered kisses on his jaw. She didn't recall ever feeling such happiness, and she gave herself up to it completely. She leaned back, her arms looped around his neck. Past his head she could see the sun low in the west. "I'll marry you, Ben, anytime, anyplace, anywhere."

She felt him tremble, and she tightened her arms around him and held him close until the trembling passed, standing there in the middle of Buena Suerte Canyon Road.

Now everything would be all right. Once they were married, Ben would have the money he needed to keep his land. Together they'd make a life rich in happiness and love.

Tomorrow night, after the realtor's ball, she'd tell him everything.

THE PEBBLED DRIVE at the Summerhill Elks Lodge crunched beneath their feet as Ben and Juliana walked toward the entrance. The lodge was the only facility in the city large enough for an event the size of the annual realtors' ball.

Juliana clung to Ben's arm, her hand—her whole body—shaking. "I feel absolutely light-headed without my wig," she whispered as they fell into line behind several other late arrivals. "Are you sure I look all right?"

All right? Ben smiled down at her, feeling such love and pride that it frightened him. She'd twisted a silvery cord through her short brown hair, which curved over her cheeks and forehead in silky tendrils. She looked sensational in the gray gauze dress they'd bought that fateful day at the mall. She worried at a long string of pearls with one hand, rubbing the creamy spheres together without regard for their delicacy. He was so proud of her that it even made it worth the effort of crawling into a tuxedo again.

"Hell no!" he said. "You don't look all right—you look great." He bent swiftly and kissed her on the lips.

She yanked away, her face flushing, but not before he'd felt her response. He grinned and winked.

"Don't do that," she exclaimed. "What will people think?"

"That I'm crazy about you. Maybe they'll think there's something going on between us. A smart few might think we're engaged."

She groaned. "Have you noticed a certain tendency in me to overlook the forest for the trees?"

"Now that you mention it. . . ." He raised one eyebrow and guided her inside the foyer ablaze with lights. It was probably going out in public for the first time without the wig, he decided. She'd be all right as soon as this affair got underway.

"JULIANA, you look wonderful!"

Juliana turned to exchange pleasantries with a gray-haired, jewel-bedecked woman, leaning forward to kiss the air over her shoulder. It had been this way all evening; everyone genuinely happy to see Juliana out and about. She'd been hugged, kissed and patted ever since she walked into the building.

"Well, you certainly don't look as if you've been ill," the woman exclaimed. "You look radiant, in fact. Short hair's in, you know. You . . ."

Juliana's smile slipped; across the room she saw Barbara Snell.

Escorted by Cary Goddard. Her grip on Ben's arm tightened.

Well of course, she'd be here, Juliana reminded herself. She'd be winning heaven only knows how many honors tonight. But did she have to come with Cary? Did she have to flaunt it?

Barbara glanced up, and her gaze met Juliana's—met and locked. After a long hesitation, Barbara smiled and waved; she spoke to Cary and he also looked Juliana's way and nodded.

But she had seen that expression on Barbara's face, cutting through all the phony "nice" the woman used like a net to snare the unwary. Juliana made a silent vow to avoid Barbara, at all costs.

A tap on the shoulder brought Juliana swinging around. A waiter stood there, holding a tray of champagne glasses. "Mrs. Robinson?" he asked. "Mrs. Juliana Robinson?"

"Yes?"

"Telephone." He gestured toward the entryway.

Juliana excused herself, trying not to let her concern show. Who would call her here?

Pete. "Am I glad I got you," he exclaimed.

She felt sick with dread. "What's the matter?"

"Barbara's asking questions."

She controlled her impatience. "You're going to have to be a little more specific than that, Pete."

There was a pause. Then he said caustically, "Okay, how's this for specific? Barbara has a cousin who works for the Summerhill Trust and Realty Company."

Juliana felt as if a hole had opened up beneath her feet. "Are you sure?"

"Pretty sure. Here's what happened—Barbara came in for lunch at Señor Pizza today, and of course I stopped by her table. We're dishing the bull and she says to me, sweet as pie, 'I hear you're buying a piece of Ben Ware's land.'"

"Oh, no."

"Oh, yes. With my usual savoir faire, I stuttered and stammered and finally asked her where she got her information. She politely suggested it was none of my business."

"Pete, get to the point. How does that tell you she has connections with Summerhill Trust?"

"Because I mentioned it later to Sandy and *she* told me. See, our neighbor's daughter dates Barbara's son and when she was looking for a job, he told her to go see his mother's cousin at Summerhill Trust."

Juliana groaned. "Now you tell me."

"Hey, I have no intention of being left holding the bag all by my lonesome."

She couldn't blame him for that. When the conversation ended, she stood there for a moment, thinking. All she had to do was avoid Barbara tonight, Juliana decided. Tomorrow Ben would know everything and then it wouldn't matter.

That proved easier said than done. A few minutes later, Barbara followed Juliana into the women's lounge.

Barbara made the opening gambit. "Well, don't you look nice."

"Thank you. So do you."

Barbara smoothed the skirt of her black cocktail dress over ample hips. "So I guess that takes care of the amenities. Juliana, about Ben's land—do you know what he's decided to do? My client's getting impatient."

"Cary—your client's name is Cary." Juliana spoke more sharply than she intended and tried to moderate her tone.

"Let me give you a piece of advice about Ben." She put her hand on the door and met the other woman's level gaze. "Don't push him. You do and he'll push back."

"I wouldn't have to push him if a certain party hadn't come in with some cockamamie proposal to delay the inevitable."

Juliana recoiled. She'd never seen Barbara come so close to losing it. "The land is Ben's, not mine. If you're smart, you won't bother him about this tonight."

The lounge door swung open and a bevy of talking, laughing women trooped inside. In the ensuing confusion, Juliana made her getaway.

Physically, at least. Mentally she couldn't shake the feeling of doom caused by Barbara's hostility. If she'd ferreted out Pete's name, then she'd know the rest, whether she could prove it or not. Pete's precarious finances were no secret in this town.

But even so, she can't prove anything, Juliana told herself defiantly. *If she says anything to Ben, I'll just brazen it out.*

"Let's dance."

Ben's voice in her ear made her jump. Gratefully she turned into his strong arms. She'd tell him the very minute they got home. Preferably in bed. She smiled into his tuxedo-clad shoulder.

He glanced down at her. "Huh?"

"Just thinking. About you . . . and me . . . and a nice little engagement party for just the two of us, when we can get out of here."

His hands on her tightened, and his blue eyes narrowed. "Not *too* little," he said in that smoky voice that sent shivers up and down her spine.

She settled back into the rhythm of the music, but her thoughts kept crowding in. She'd made a mistake, trying to manipulate him with her money, even if it was for his own good. Besides, now that they were going to get married, he wouldn't be so stubborn about the money issue.

Would he?

The music ended and they moved toward the buffet table, hand in hand. Ben leaned down and spoke in her ear so she could hear him despite the drone of voices. "Do we have to stay for the awards?" He gave her hand a meaningful squeeze.

"I don't see why. It's not as if I expect to win anything," she said dryly.

He gave her a grin ripe with promise and turned for the door, but she pulled back. "Wait a minute. If I don't stay, it'll look like sour grapes. I'm sorry."

He tilted his carefully barbered head and sighed. "Sorrier than you know. I was thinking chandeliers and mirrors, but if saving face is more important—"

"Not leaving so soon?" Barbara's voice announced her arrival, Cary at her side. He included both Ben and Juliana in a curt nod of greeting.

"We have other plans," Ben said, one brow arching up. "Got another party to go to."

"What a shame." Barbara drew Cary forward and slipped her arm beneath his, clinging to him. "Before you go, Ben, I wonder if you could give me just the teeniest little hint about how you're going to respond to the last offer I brought you for your land."

"Why, I—" Ben broke off abruptly, his brow wrinkling and his eyes narrowing. He looked from Barbara to Cary and back again.

He knows, Juliana suddenly realized. *He's just figured it out. Heaven help us.*

A mask seemed to drop over Ben's face, which only an instant before had been relaxed and smiling. He ignored

Barbara and gave Cary Goddard a simmering look. "The answer's no, Goddard. The answer's always going to be no to you."

Barbara gasped. "I'm not representing Mr. Goddard. My client is—"

"Let it go." Cary's sleek voice cut her off in mid-sentence. "It was a good try, but it didn't work. Now we've got to figure out what will."

"*She* told him!" Barbara's little-girl facade split open to reveal a furious woman. "Of all the nerve!"

Ben frowned. "What are you talking about? Seeing you two here together just brought the whole thing into focus. Juliana didn't say anything—hell, she didn't know herself."

"Didn't she?" Barbara's vituperative words brought three pairs of eyes to bear on Juliana.

She swallowed hard. "W-why, I . . ."

Barbara took a step forward, her jaw jutting out. "Tell him, Juliana. Tell him how you ran into Cary and me at a restaurant. Tell him what you said to us."

This was Juliana's worst nightmare come true. She wanted to turn and run but felt rooted to the spot—literally. Lips parted, she stared at Barbara, incapable of speech.

Barbara suffered no such disadvantage. "And while you're at it, explain your ex-husband's part in trying to pick off a few prime acres of Ben's land."

Ben's lip curled. "Now I know you're nuts. Pete hasn't got that kind of money."

"No," Barbara agreed. "But *she* does."

People were beginning to stare, but for the first time in her life, Juliana simply didn't care about public opinion. The only opinion that mattered to her was that of Benjamin Ware.

He was looking at her with a kind of painful confusion: *Say it ain't so!* And she couldn't; she closed her eyes and drew a quivering breath, trying desperately to think what to do.

If she denied everything, what could Barbara prove? *Ben will stand by me*, Juliana tried to convince herself. *He loves me and I love him. That's enough.*

Only it wasn't. She expected honesty from him and he deserved honesty from her. Okay, she could tell him about seeing the dynamic duo at lunch and surmising the true identity of the would-be buyer of Ben's land. But how could she ever explain away using Pete as the front man for her own land deal?

With her history, who would believe she was trying to give away money? And even if Ben believed it, could he ever forgive? He, who even refused a handout from his mother?

But what if Juliana brazened it out and married him and then he learned the truth? She didn't think she could stand that, to truly have him and then lose him. If Ben asked Pete point-blank, could Pete handle a bold-faced lie?

Pete and his histrionic abilities lay somewhere in the future; at present, it was a question of Juliana's willingness to tell the man she loved a blatant lie.

She opened her eyes and looked at him. And for the first time in so very long, she saw again the raw-edged pain that had been so much a part of him before.

Before they fell in love. Before they made love. Before he proposed marriage. Before she accepted.

She lifted her eyes to his and said in a voice that was little more than a croak: "I'm sorry. Everything I did, I did because I love you."

12

BEN FELT as if he'd been poleaxed. He leaned toward her, praying he'd misunderstood. "Juliana, let's get the hell out of here. We have to talk." A sudden drum roll swallowed up his words.

The crowd milling around the tight little foursome surged forward. The awards program was about to begin in the next room.

Someone banged into Ben from behind and he stumbled, tried to catch his balance and staggered forward. He felt completely adrift and helpless, unable to assimilate what had just happened. Finally he got his feet under him again and turned toward Juliana—only she wasn't there anymore. She was gone.

The last stragglers disappeared through the doors. He was alone with Cary Goddard and Barbara Snell.

Barbara gave Ben her saccharine smile. "If Juliana had bought that land from you, she'd have resold it to Goddard Enterprises for an incredibly hefty profit. Be glad you found out in time."

Ben stared at the woman. "Found out what?"

"How she's been using you, of course." Barbara's baby-blue eyes widened with an approximation of innocent outrage. "The woman's unscrupulous in business *and* in pleasure."

"Shut up, Barbara."

Surprised, Ben blinked and turned toward Cary Goddard.

The man looked at Barbara with contempt on his face, yet his voice was curiously soft. "Run along, now," he said, dismissing the woman who stood there with mouth agape. "If you're not there, they might give all your little honors to someone less deserving."

"I—"

"*Go*, Barbara."

She did, flouncing through the doors and slamming them behind her. Goddard watched her for a moment and then turned slowly.

Looking at him now, Ben tried to remember why he felt such blind, stubborn animosity. . . and couldn't come up with any reason. At least no reason that made sense.

"Goddard, I think we've got a few things to talk about. Care to join me in the bar? I'm buying."

"You're about to pay?" Goddard's mouth turned down sardonically beneath the full mustache. "I can't tell you how long I've waited for that."

JULIANA RANG Pete's doorbell and Sandy answered. "What's happened?" she exclaimed, gesturing for Juliana to enter. "Have you been crying?"

"No." It was a lie, of course, but pride was about all Juliana had left. "Is Pete home?"

"Here, Juli."

At the sound of his voice, Juliana whirled, hands clenching at her sides. "Pete, I've got to talk to you."

He frowned and cast a questioning glance at his wife. She nodded, and without another word, left the room.

At a loss to begin, Juliana glanced around her. A comfortable room, a room where people lived. Nothing like the beautiful blue and cream living room in Juliana's house. Juliana would never allow children's toys to litter the floor, or a man to kick his shoes off under the couch.

Pete led her to the couch. "Sit down, hon. You look all done in."

She shuddered. "It hit the fan tonight," she said.

"Want to tell me about it?"

"No. But since I dragged you into all this, I thought I owed it to you." For a few minutes she sat there, giving in to the numbing sense of defeat. Pete waited patiently. At last she looked up. "Barbara confronted me at the ball tonight. When it came to the moment of truth, I just couldn't lie to Ben."

Pete sucked in his breath. "How'd he take it?"

"That's a stupid question!" she flared. "How would you take it? I'm sure he thinks I tried to get his land by nefarious means so I could make a killing by reselling it. For all I know, Ben thinks I . . . I got close to him for that very purpose."

"How close is close?"

She tried to conceal her anguish. "Don't ask." She couldn't meet his eyes. "I've really screwed everything up, but I was trying to do the right thing. I thought I'd changed so much, learned so much because of everything that's happened."

Pete's hand settled on her shoulder. "What did you learn, Juliana?"

She gave a short bitter laugh. "That even a bad haircut grows out." She ran her hand through her short brown hair.

He smiled, but didn't let her evade the real issue. "What else?"

She thought for a minute, pursing her lips. "I guess I've learned that love and happiness are more important than money and public opinion," she said slowly.

Pete's jaw dropped. His astonishment brought a faint smile to her stiff lips. "And I've learned that I'm not immortal. There may not be a tomorrow."

"Just in case there is, you'd better settle things with Ben tonight, Juli."

Despair weighed even more heavily about her shoulders. "It's hopeless. He'll never forgive me."

"How do you know? Have you groveled? What have you got to lose at this point except pride?"

Hope flared. "You think there's a chance?"

Pete looked disgusted. "How the hell would I know? All I know is that *I* believe you. Maybe Ben will, too." He laughed. "This is weird—I'm giving you advice and you're listening."

She pressed her hands together in her lap. "Our marriage must have been hell for you," she said. It was a new thought. Up until now, she'd always thought of the marriage in terms of her own disapppointment.

"Yeah, it was, part of the time. Most of the time. But there were good times, too. Good and bad, it's all over now."

"Yes." She stood up. "Did I ever thank you for your kindness while I was in the hospital?"

"No. But no thanks are necessary."

"You're wrong. *Thank you* and *I'm sorry* and *I love you* are words that should be said more often."

"More often than *listing* and *commission* and *sold*?" he teased.

He stood up and she put her arms around him. "I'm sorry," she whispered. "For everything. And I thank you, also for everything." She kissed his cheek. "And I love you. You gave me a wonderful daughter and ten years of your life. All I ever gave you was a hard time and an inferiority complex."

"Yeah, but it didn't stick." He pulled back and smiled. "You have learned a lot, Juli, and changed a lot. I hope Ben is man enough to realize it."

She tried to laugh. "I'm afraid what he'll realize is that I've been playing volleyball without a net." She caught her lower lip between her teeth until she regained control. "We went to the party in my car. He drove, and I took off without the key. I walked here—can you give me a ride?"

He reached into his pocket and pulled out a cluster of keys. "Take my car," he said. "You can return it tomorrow." He unclipped a key and handed it to her.

"Thanks."

"You going home?"

"I don't know. I honestly don't know." She paused with her hand on the doorknob. "I've got to find a place to do some serious thinking."

LIGHTS BURNED in the windows of Juliana's house, so Ben pulled into the driveway. He jumped out of the Mercedes and sprinted to the door.

"Juliana!" He pounded with his fists, putting his shoulders into it. "Open up!"

The door swung wide and Paige stood there, frowning. "Are you crazy? It's the middle of the night!"

"Oh, it's you." He peered over her shoulder. "I want to talk to your mother."

"She isn't here. I thought she'd be with you. Wasn't the ball tonight?" She stepped aside for him to enter. She wore creased khaki-colored trousers and a safari shirt and she looked tired.

"I didn't know you were home." He hesitated inside the living room, looking around.

"We got back a day early." She stifled a yawn. "You look gorgeous." She ran an appreciative glance over him. "So where's Mother?"

"Damned if I know. There was a . . . let's call it a scene. She took off, and when I saw the lights I thought she'd come home."

"Well, she didn't."

Ben glowered at the girl. "You don't seem overly alarmed."

"She's a big girl, in case you hadn't noticed." She shrugged elaborately. "I'm beat. I'm going to bed. Lock up when you leave, okay?"

She left him standing there.

"WAKE UP, DAMMIT!" Ben pounded on Pete's front door, stepping back every few seconds to peer toward the wing where the bedrooms were located. Finally a light came on. After another interval of frenzied pounding, the door swung open.

Pete stood there, weaving groggily. "Judas Priest, Ben, pipe down, will'ya?"

"Have you seen Juliana?"

Pete stifled a yawn. "Sure. Lots of times."

"Everybody's a friggin' comedian!"

Ben's roar seemed to shock Pete awake. Into the sudden silence, a soft, scared voice called out from the darkness inside. "Honey, what is it? What's wrong?"

"See what you've done." Pete started to close the door. "You woke Sandy."

"Daddy, who is it?"

"Now you woke the boys. Go home, Ben. This is no time of night to come calling."

"Dammit, Pete!" Ben stuck his toe out to stop the door from closing in his face. "All I want to know is whether or not you've seen her tonight."

"Yes! I loaned her a car. Now go home and let me get some sleep." Pete banged the door against the intrusive toe. When Ben jerked back, the door slammed with a decisive click.

Ben stood there, angry and thwarted. And only then did he realize that he hadn't asked Pete a single question about his alleged part in the great land rip-off.

Some things were just more important than others.

JULIANA SAT in darkness in Ben's kitchen and waited. And so, she thought, it all came down to this. The very course of her life hinged on the outcome of the next few hours . . . maybe even the next few minutes.

She felt numb helplessness, as if events were out of her hands and speeding at a breakneck pace toward some conclusion beyond her control. He had so many reasons to turn against her, and only one to turn toward her.

He would have to take her on face value or not at all. On faith . . . on blind trust . . . on love.

At that moment she loved Benjamin Ware more than she had dreamed possible. A future without him was unthinkable, yet she found it impossible to believe he could forgive her for deceiving him. If the tables were turned, could she forgive him?

She hoped so—she believed so—but how could she ever be sure? Changing was so *damned* hard. Being a reformed person took almost as much effort as preserving liberty—the price of both was unceasing vigilance.

She folded her arms on the tabletop and lowered her head with a sigh. How to explain the way things turn out? If the aneurysm had ruptured as she drove her car along the freeway or while she was home alone, she probably would not have survived. But it had happened here, in Ben's kitchen. And being the kind of man he was, he couldn't just take her to the hospital and wash his hands of her.

Later, he had pushed and prodded and forced her back into the mainstream. When she faltered, he was there, a steady presence she'd grown to trust implicitly.

"Don't depend on me, because I can't protect you," he said once, but she'd depended upon him anyway, because she'd had to. And he had protected her . . . from loneliness, from self-doubt, but most of all, from giving up.

She shuddered. She saw the person she had been in a far different light, now. What she had called confidence she now classified as arrogance. What she'd considered a professional attitude now seemed mere impatience. And what she'd believed to be self-sufficiency had turned out to be a fear of commitment resulting in years of loneliness.

It had taken a catastrophic illness to penetrate the rigid shell of her conceit. She'd survived, but not intact—the violation of her brain had left her with a shaven skull and memory glitches that magnified her vulnerability. But in another sense, it had made her aware of her humanity.

Through it all, Ben was there. And she had fallen in love with him.

Why hadn't she tried to lie her way out of this? She'd asked herself that question over and over again. The old Juliana would have, not because she enjoyed lying, but because the stakes were high enough to justify it. The new Juliana couldn't have lived with herself.

Immersed in her own misery, she felt the weight of a hand settle on her head. She gave a little cry and bolted upright in her chair.

Ben stood there, a darker shape in the dark room. She didn't need to hear his voice or see him to identify him; the energy that surged from the palm of his hand into her scalp was enough.

"Please," she whispered. "I'm sorry I deceived you."

"Don't explain." His naturally gravelly voice sounded even rougher and deeper. He slipped his hand down over her skull to the back of her neck and drew her to her feet.

He's going to throw me bodily out of here, she thought wildly. She had never felt such leashed intensity in his touch, and her heart leaped and plunged wildly. She licked her lips, searching for words that could make a difference.

"You've got to give me a chance, Ben." She hated the trembling note of panic in her voice. Somehow she had to make him listen. She would even take Pete's advice and grovel—anything, anything at all to make him understand. "Everything I did I did because—"

"Shut up." He pulled her against him, holding her there with one hand at the back of her head, the other at her waist. "There's nothing you can say that will make a difference."

"Don't say that!" She grabbed the lapels of his tuxedo and hung on. "You've got to—"

"Will you shut up?"

He wrapped his arms around her and pressed his face into the curve of her neck. For a moment she stood there, too surprised and confused to understand. He held her so tightly that she felt the vibration of his heartbeat, heard the ragged intake of his breath.

Trembling and uncertain, yet determined to dare, she slipped her arms beneath his and slid her hands up his back, wanting to hold him in her embrace forever.

He sighed. "That's better. Now I'm going to be adult about this and give you a choice. Do you want to talk or— what the hell. I'm *not* going to give you a choice."

He leaned forward and tumbled her over his shoulder and stood up. His sudden action knocked the breath out of her and she dangled, bent at the hips, across his broad shoulder. Her breasts pressed against his back.

She stiffened. "What are you doing?" she cried. "You said I had a choice!"

"I lied." He carried her into the bedroom. His hand slipped beneath the gray gauze skirt to stroke up her silken legs and she stifled a groan.

He dumped her on the bed and leaned over to switch on the light. She stared up at him, her breath catching at the lusty expression on his face.

She struggled to sit up. "Wait a minute," she pleaded breathlessly. "We can't do this—not until you understand why I've acted so stupid."

"Stupid?" He yanked off his bow tie and tossed it aside. The tuxedo jacket followed. "Is it stupid to love someone enough to try to help them whether they want help or not?" He spoke fiercely but not angrily. "Parents do that all the time. Didn't your folks ever say to you, 'You'll thank me for this some day'?"

"Of course, but I never believed them."

She couldn't tear her mesmerized gaze away from him as he snapped the suspenders off his shoulders. He kicked off his shoes and dropped the suspenders around his hips. Swearing impatiently, he fought the buttons of his shirt, his task made harder because he watched her and not what he was doing.

He tossed the shirt aside. "Damn but you're a stubborn woman!" He dropped to his knees on the bed beside her. He didn't touch her, just stared into her eyes. "Do you love me?" he asked in a voice more gentle than any she'd ever heard from him.

"Oh, yes. Yes, I love you. That's why I—"

"I love you, too," he said. "That's all that's important, at the moment. Shut up and kiss me."

She had never received a command with such joy. She rose to a sitting position on the bed, jerky as a puppet on a string, and slid her arms around his neck. Her eyes asked a question—*Am I dreaming?*

He answered her with a slow, soft smile.

She touched his mouth with hers, lightly at first, gentle kisses that quickly moved on to something else. A familiar pleasure began to build inside her and she sighed and opened her mouth to him.

His tongue plunged between her lips, even as his hands manipulated the zipper down the back of her dress. Without interrupting the kiss, he slipped the garment off her shoulders and down around her waist.

She clung to him weakly, content to draw from his strength. All she desired was to be one with him. He laid her back gently on the bed, undressing her so skillfully that she scarcely knew what was happening.

She felt drunk, not with alcohol but with a heady combination of relief and desire. He loved her without reservation, as she loved him. He loved her enough to take her on faith, and she loved him enough to give herself on faith.

He lay beside her and the mattress shifted beneath his weight. He took her in his arms, his body hard and hot against hers. "Open your eyes," he commanded, then added a gentle "please."

Slowly she complied. His beloved features swam before her dazzled eyes. He stroked her collarbone lightly with his fingers, then moved his hand down her body with languorous strokes. Pausing at one breast, he applied gentle pressure, lifting the firm weight in his palm, tugging the nipple between curved fingers.

He raised his head, his possessive gaze locked with her rapt one. She held her breath as he lowered his head to her breast and took the nipple between his lips.

She groaned and pressed her head back on the pillow. Eyes closed, she savored the sensations created by his mouth. With his hand, he stroked down across her stomach. She tensed and her thighs trembled in anticipation of his touch in the cluster of dark curls. When it came she let out her breath in a long, languorous sigh.

Everything was happening so fast. Her body tightened and she felt the tension spiral until she knew she'd never be able to withstand it. She covered his undulating hand with her own trembling fingers and groaned his name.

He lifted his head and smiled at her in perfect understanding, his blond hair damp across his forehead and his blue eyes blazing a question. She couldn't speak; she nodded, and he understood.

As he moved over her, as his body found hers moist and ready, she understood at last what it was to give herself, emotionally as well as physically.

She wasn't afraid anymore, not of living, not of dying . . . not of loving.

Especially not of loving.

THEY LAY IN THE FOUR-POSTER, apart and yet more together than they'd ever been. Only their hands touched, yet they were one.

Juliana rolled her head to the side so she could see his face. He looked sleepy and satisfied. She squeezed his hand. "I love you," she whispered.

He turned his head and smiled lazily. "Ditto."

She lifted his hand to her lips and kissed his palm. "I guess we ought to talk now," she forced herself to say.

"Hey, I don't bite . . . much." He rolled onto his side and leaned over to drop a quick kiss on the upper swell of her breast. "Okay, say your piece. I'm listening."

Her lips tightened and she swallowed hard. "This is hard," she said finally.

His smile encouraged her. "If it's worth having, etcetera. . . ."

She nodded. "I guess I might as well plunge right in, then." She sucked in a deep breath. "Everything I did, I did because I wanted to *help* you," she said in a rush. "I wanted

to loan you the money you needed—hell, I wanted to *give*
you the money."

"And I wouldn't even talk about it—I know. And I
called *you* stubborn," he said with an unrepentant air.

She silenced him with a disapproving frown. "And then
I found out Cary was behind the second offer." She looked
into his eyes, willing him to understand and believe.

He pressed her palm against his chest and dragged it
down until it lay flat on his stomach, her fingers splayed
and pointing down like arrows. "Why didn't you just tell
me?" he asked.

"By the time I found out, it was too late. You needed a
buyer and I didn't see anyone else coming forward."
Ashamed because she hadn't been honest with him, she
dropped her gaze. "It's not that I lacked faith in you." She
pressed the pads of her fingers into his muscular flesh.

He tensed and gave a soft grunt. "Okay. Assuming
you're right...."

"You know I'm right." She snaked her hands lower,
curling her fingers through his crisp thick hair until her
fingers encountered the resistance they sought. "So I came
up with that ill-conceived plan to give you the money you
needed by buying a few acres. I wasn't in cahoots with
Cary, I swear."

He gulped, his body going stiff in all directions. "I believe you," he croaked.

She slipped her fingers around the powerful thrust of
him with gentle insistence. "But now everything's
changed."

"Jeez, you'll have to tell me. I'm not thinking straight."
He closed his eyes briefly, but he didn't attempt to dis-
courage the attentions of her hand.

"Well, this is California, after all. Assuming you're a
man of your word and you still plan to make an honest
woman of me—"

"Ah, that it could be done," he moaned.

She ignored the interruption. "Yes, well, if you do the right thing by me, good old community property comes into the picture. What's mine is yours and what's yours is mine."

"Hold it." He clamped his hand around her wrist and his blue eyes blazed. "What's mine is yours and what's yours is yours." He shook his head and frowned. "Let me take another crack at that. What's mine is yours and what's yours is—"

She rolled over until her face was only inches from his. "Do you know how ridiculous that sounds, my darling?"

He assumed an indignant air, with some difficulty, she noted. "I wouldn't say exactly ridiculous. More like . . . stupid."

"Okay. *Stupid* works for me."

"It's just that . . . we've got to live on my income."

"Why? Who's going to live on mine?"

"You're twisting my words."

"That's not all I'm twisting." Her second hand joined her first.

"Jeez, slow down or I won't be able to . . . maintain—" he begged. He swallowed hard.

"All right, if you insist." She slowed the smooth pull of her hands. "Anyway, we can keep this place if you want to. If you want to be an avocado farmer it's all right with me. Anything's all right with me."

"You mean that?"

"Of course."

"Then you won't mind that I sort of made a deal with Cary Goddard."

She sat bolt upright in the middle of the bed. "After all the hell I've been through, you sold to Cary Goddard?"

He lay on his back looking up at her. "After you ran out on me tonight, I realized something. My own pride got me into this mess, not anything you did or didn't do."

"But—"

"Let me say this and get it over with, okay?" He glowered at her and she subsided. "Everything was all mixed up in my head, as if Cary Goddard was somehow responsible for my mother's death and my own inadequacies. And then I got tangled up with you...."

"Tangled up? That hardly does me justice!" She suppressed a grin.

But he was serious. "You've been sick, Juliana—no one knows that better than I do. I didn't want to take advantage of you, and I sure as hell didn't want to fall in love with you. I did both."

She leaned down and touched the side of his face with awful longing. "For which I'll be eternally grateful. I love you, but I also need you. Without you, I'd still be a shark in the ocean of real estate. I count on you to keep me ... well, maybe not honest—I think I may have taken a bum rap on that—but *nice*."

His eyes widened suddenly, as if he'd just remembered something important. "Speaking of nice...."

He rolled over to the edge of the bed and stood up. She watched his bare backside with appreciation as he walked buck naked out the door. She didn't even ask where he was going; instead she anticipated his return.

In seconds he was back, and the front view was even nicer than the back one. So intent was she upon admiring his powerful body that she didn't notice he carried something in his hands, until he thrust it toward her.

"What's this?" She shifted her glance, brows arching.

"Congratulations. Tonight you were named Summerhill real estate's Good Samaritan."

"You're kidding!" She took the plaque and read the heading: The Webster Malone Good Samaritan Award. "Is this a joke?"

"Nope. Remember the Burtons? They've apparently been an albatross for a long time. You took them out of circulation and your fellow real-estate professionals are appropriately grateful."

Juliana shook her head. "This is crazy. They were a little difficult, but once we understood each other, it was a piece of cake."

"Kind of tells you something about the level of good deeds in real-estate circles, then, doesn't it?" Ben dropped down beside her on the bed. "The best part is, Barbara nominated you, back when she thought she could afford to be magnanimous."

"Now I *know* you're putting me on!" She stared at him, her astonishment complete.

"I'm not! Stella thinks Babs was just trying to humiliate you as an also-ran. Then when she found out about that back-door deal you made with Pete, she tried to withdraw your name and got turned down flat. Seems Stella had given the awards committee chapter and verse on a number of good deeds you'd quietly done over the past several years. So you can take the prize and be happy. In my opinion, you earned it."

"No, I didn't. But I will next year." Choked up, she brushed at the moisture on her cheeks. *I hope you're proud of me at last, Daddy,* she thought. She hugged the plaque to her. "I suppose Barbara was named Summerhill Real Estate Star for the umpteenth time." She didn't feel the expected twinge and realized it simply didn't matter to her anymore.

"Yeah, but she won't be next year. I told Goddard we could deal, but not through that bitch. He's going to use—"

"Not me!" Juliana's fingers convulsed around the award, her eyes widening with horror.

"Settle down. You think I'm crazy?" He gave her an offended glance. "Somebody else. Anybody else. *You'll* be representing me—I mean us."

"I don't know...."

"That way we'll save the commission," he wheedled.

She gave him a look so richly appalled that he burst out laughing. "Any more questions?"

"Only one. Why are you so willing to believe in me? Even Pete thought at first that I was trying to get control of your land. Even I have to admit I don't look too good in all this."

He thought about it for a moment. Then he asked, "Do you remember when Barbara accused you of conspiring to cheat that widow?"

"How could I forget? It was one of the blacker moments in my life."

He nodded. "And remember, I had faith in you, even though you thought you were probably guilty."

"That's right, you did." She gazed at him, her heart filled with wonder.

"My love, there was an explanation then, and I knew there was an explanation now. I guess that's what love does—makes you goofy enough to trust. But even if there hadn't been an explanation, I wouldn't have turned my back on you."

"You wouldn't?" She could barely believe her luck in finding a man like this one. "What would you have done?"

"Worked harder to convince you that you could trust me and count on me. Baby, I've been dodging responsibility ever since my wife—my *first* wife—died. But not anymore. I'm committed to you, for better or for worse."

"For richer or poorer," she whispered.

He hesitated. A slight smile touched his lips. "For richer or poorer," he agreed finally.

"I love you."

"I love you, too."

They melted together in an embrace that promised an endless future of love and happiness, for at last Juliana dared to believe such possibilities existed.

And with Ben's last coherent thought, he promised himself that tomorrow he'd explain to her that he and Cary Goddard had reached a meeting of the minds that would bring each of them half of what he wanted. Goddard would buy twelve acres of the Ware avocado ranch, which would get Lillian out of the avocado business, but leave Ben with a decent-sized operation, plus a little money to invest in his security business. He wouldn't be rich—any extra bucks would go to the shelters in San Francisco and Los Angeles that had helped give him his second chance.

Because he'd had that second chance, he'd been around to help Juliana seize her own. In that flashing instant before he gave himself up to his love for her, he realized that he would take not only a second chance on her but a third and a fifth and a tenth, if that's what it required.

Chances beyond counting, all in the name of love.

You'll flip . . . your pages won't!
Read paperbacks *hands-free* with

Book Mate • I

The perfect "mate" for all your romance paperbacks

Traveling • Vacationing • At Work • In Bed • Studying
• Cooking • Eating

Perfect size for all standard paperbacks, this wonderful invention makes reading a pure pleasure! Ingenious design holds paperback books OPEN and FLAT so even wind can't ruffle pages— leaves your hands free to do other things. Reinforced, wipe-clean vinyl-covered holder flexes to let you turn pages without undoing the strap . . . supports paperbacks so well, they have the strength of hardcovers!

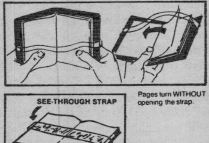

Pages turn WITHOUT opening the strap.

SEE-THROUGH STRAP

Reinforced back stays flat.

Built in bookmark

BOOK MARK

BACK COVER HOLDING STRIP

10˝ x 7¼˝, opened.
Snaps closed for easy carrying, too.

PASSPORT TO ROMANCE VACATION SWEEPSTAKES

OFFICIAL RULES

SWEEPSTAKES RULES AND REGULATIONS. NO PURCHASE NECESSARY.

HOW TO ENTER:

1. To enter, complete this official entry form and return with your invoice in the envelope provided, or print your name, address, telephone number and age on a plain piece of paper and mail to: Passport to Romance, P.O. Box #1397, Buffalo, N.Y. 14269-1397. No mechanically reproduced entries accepted.
2. All entries must be received by the Contest Closing Date, midnight, December 31, 1990 to be eligible.
3. Prizes: There will be ten (10) Grand Prizes awarded, each consisting of a choice of a trip for two people to: i) London, England (approximate retail value $5,050 U.S.); ii) England, Wales and Scotland (approximate retail value $6,400 U.S.); iii) Caribbean Cruise (approximate retail value $7,300 U.S.); iv) Hawaii (approximate retail value $ 9,550 U.S.); v) Greek Island Cruise in the Mediterranean (approximate retail value $12,250 U.S.); vi) France (approximate retail value $7,300 U.S.).
4. Any winner may choose to receive any trip or a cash alternative prize of $5,000.00 U.S. in lieu of the trip.
5. Odds of winning depend on number of entries received.
6. A random draw will be made by Nielsen Promotion Services, an independent judging organization on January 29, 1991, in Buffalo, N.Y., at 11:30 a.m. from all eligible entries received on or before the Contest Closing Date. Any Canadian entrants who are selected must correctly answer a time-limited, mathematical skill-testing question in order to win. Quebec residents may submit any litigation respecting the conduct and awarding of a prize in this contest to the Régie des loteries et courses du Quebec.
7. Full contest rules may be obtained by sending a stamped, self-addressed envelope to: "Passport to Romance Rules Request", P.O. Box 9998, Saint John, New Brunswick, E2L 4N4.
8. Payment of taxes other than air and hotel taxes is the sole responsibility of the winner.
9. Void where prohibited by law.

PASSPORT TO ROMANCE VACATION SWEEPSTAKES

OFFICIAL RULES

SWEEPSTAKES RULES AND REGULATIONS. NO PURCHASE NECESSARY.

HOW TO ENTER:

1. To enter, complete this official entry form and return with your invoice in the envelope provided, or print your name, address, telephone number and age on a plain piece of paper and mail to: Passport to Romance, P.O. Box #1397, Buffalo, N.Y. 14269-1397. No mechanically reproduced entries accepted.
2. All entries must be received by the Contest Closing Date, midnight, December 31, 1990 to be eligible.
3. Prizes: There will be ten (10) Grand Prizes awarded, each consisting of a choice of a trip for two people to: i) London, England (approximate retail value $5,050 U.S.); ii) England, Wales and Scotland (approximate retail value $6,400 U.S.); iii) Caribbean Cruise (approximate retail value $7,300 U.S.); iv) Hawaii (approximate retail value $ 9,550 U.S.); v) Greek Island Cruise in the Mediterranean (approximate retail value $12,250 U.S.); vi) France (approximate retail value $7,300 U.S.).
4. Any winner may choose to receive any trip or a cash alternative prize of $5,000.00 U.S. in lieu of the trip.
5. Odds of winning depend on number of entries received.
6. A random draw will be made by Nielsen Promotion Services, an independent judging organization on January 29, 1991, in Buffalo, N.Y., at 11:30 a.m. from all eligible entries received on or before the Contest Closing Date. Any Canadian entrants who are selected must correctly answer a time-limited, mathematical skill-testing question in order to win. Quebec residents may submit any litigation respecting the conduct and awarding of a prize in this contest to the Régie des loteries et courses du Quebec.
7. Full contest rules may be obtained by sending a stamped, self-addressed envelope to: "Passport to Romance Rules Request", P.O. Box 9998, Saint John, New Brunswick, E2L 4N4.
8. Payment of taxes other than air and hotel taxes is the sole responsibility of the winner.
9. Void where prohibited by law.

RLS-DIR

VACATION SWEEPSTAKES

Official Entry Form

Yes, enter me in the drawing for one of ten Vacations-for-Two! If I'm a winner, I'll get my choice of any of the six different destinations being offered — and I won't have to decide until after I'm notified!

Return entries with invoice in envelope provided along with Daily Travel Allowance Voucher. Each book in your shipment has two entry forms — and the more you enter, the better your chance of winning!

Name _____

Address _____ Apt. _____

City _____ State/Prov. _____ Zip/Postal Code _____

Daytime phone number _____
                              Area Code

☐ I am enclosing a Daily Travel
Allowance Voucher in the amount of $ _____ Write in amount
                                   revealed beneath scratch-off

© 1990 HARLEQUIN ENTERPRISES LTD.

VACATION SWEEPSTAKES

MONTH 1 ENTRY

Official Entry Form

Yes, enter me in the drawing for one of ten Vacations-for-Two! If I'm a winner, I'll get my choice of any of the six different destinations being offered — and I won't have to decide until after I'm notified!

Return entries with invoice in envelope provided along with Daily Travel Allowance Voucher. Each book in your shipment has two entry forms — and the more you enter, the better your chance of winning!

Name _____

Address _____ Apt. _____

City _____ State/Prov. _____ Zip/Postal Code _____

Daytime phone number _____
                              Area Code

☐ I am enclosing a Daily Travel
Allowance Voucher in the amount of $ _____ Write in amount
                                   revealed beneath scratch-off

CPS-ONE